Best Friends

(Until Someone Better Comes Along)

Erin Downing

ALADDIN M!X

New York London Toronto Sydney New Delhi

This book is a work of fiction. Any references to historical events, real people, or real places are used fictitiously. Other names, characters, places, and events are products of the author's imagination, and any resemblance to actual events or places or persons, living or dead, is entirely coincidental.

ALADDIN M!X
Simon & Schuster Children's Publishing Division
1230 Avenue of the Americas, New York, NY 10020
First Aladdin M!X edition April 2014
Text copyright © 2014 by Erin Downing
Cover illustration copyright © 2014 by Helen Huang
Book design by Jeanine Henderson
All rights reserved, including the right of reproduction in
whole or in part in any form.
ALADDIN is a trademark of Simon & Schuster, Inc.,
and related logo is a registered trademark of Simon & Schuster, Inc.
ALADDIN M!X and related logo are registered
trademarks of Simon & Schuster, Inc.
For information about special discounts for bulk purchases,
please contact Simon & Schuster Special Sales at 1-866-506-1949
or business@simonandschuster.com.
The Simon & Schuster Speakers Bureau can bring authors to your live event.
For more information or to book an event contact the
Simon & Schuster Speakers Bureau at 1-866-248-3049
or visit our website at www.simonspeakers.com.
The text of this book was set in ITC Berkeley Oldstyle.
Manufactured in the United States of America 0314 OFF
2 4 6 8 10 9 7 5 3 1
Library of Congress Control Number 2013930315
ISBN 978-1-4424-8519-8 (pbk)
ISBN 978-1-4424-8520-4 (eBook)

For Sarah (Goese) Dockter—the best friend I was lucky to find in fourth grade, who has stuck by me ever since. No one better could ever come along.

Acknowledgments

My books are a team effort. I get lonely, I get stuck . . . and then I beg my friends and family to listen and help and read things many times. Thank you to everyone who pitched in on this novel, especially:

My fun and fabulous editor, Fiona Simpson, who wanted a book about a mean girl and thought of sweet little ol' me.

The gang at Simon & Schuster—especially Bethany Buck, Katherine Devendorf, and Jeanine Henderson—who have been so kind to me. I'm glad we're doing a book together, guys.

My savvy agent, Michael Bourret, who entertains me with his stories and amazes me with his smarts.

My friends—in particular Sarah Dockter, Jennifer Gels, Christy Lukasewycz, Catherine Clark, Barb Soderberg, and Carey Lyle—who helped me come up with Izzy's escapades, assisted with plotting, and fed and entertained me while I was writing this story. Also Robin Wasserman, who boosts my confidence every time I start to worry that I'll never finish another book.

My husband, Greg, who reads all my books many times,

even when I'm working on a book about a twelve-year-old mean girl.

My kids, who hug me extra when I'm on deadline. Though you're little now, you will all be in middle school someday. When that day comes, I hope you find friends like Bailey and Ava . . . the kind of friends who stick by you even when you make mistakes and say stupid things, because that's what great friends do. I also hope that you will always be nice to people. It's so much more fun than being mean.

Finally, thank you for reading this book. I love hearing from readers, so please let me know what you think of the book!

Chapter One

Pine trees blurred into a green mess outside the window of my mom's car as we sped along a bumpy old road to the middle of nowhere. I rolled down my window and inhaled deeply.

Ew!

I scrunched my nose into a tight little ball and blew out, trying to force the stink back out of my body. Pressing the button to roll my window up again, I flopped back against the leather seat. I'd assumed it would smell pine fresh outside, like cleaning products or candles. But it didn't. It smelled nasty. It almost felt like I could *taste* the stink in the air, it was that bad.

"I hope this isn't the 'fresh wilderness air' you've been

promising me for the past month. It smells like excrement."
I smirked, waiting for my mother's response. She should
love my use of such a big word—excrement. It was a big,
complicated word. A smart-person's word.

"Don't be rude, Isabella." My mom, Sara Hurst-
Caravelli, glanced at me in the rearview mirror. Then she
focused her eyes back on the road.

"I'm not trying to be rude," I protested. "I'm trying to
be honest. You're always telling me to expand my vocabulary. And wouldn't we all agree that 'smells like excrement'
is better than saying 'smells like—'"

"That's enough," she snapped. My mother, she of
rose-colored pedicures and coffee-shop lattes, had somehow become even crabbier as we got closer and closer to
the end of the earth. It was sort of shocking that she could
get any crabbier, but I guess a forced wilderness vacation
can do that to anyone. "And I'll thank you in advance for
your change in attitude."

I rolled the window down an inch and sniffed the
air again—delicately this time. I figured I ought to give it
another chance, just to be fair, but I immediately rolled it
back up. It really did smell terrible outside, like something
had died and was left to rot by the side of the road. I leaned

my head against the glass and stared up into the canopy of pine trees that now hung low and dark around our car. Even though it was only four in the afternoon, it was as dim as twilight inside the shadowed forest. Almost like the trees could sense my mood.

"Isn't this beautiful?" My dad, Alex, mused from the passenger seat. It sounded like he was reading a line off a script. I knew he was about as big a fan of the woods as the rest of us, but he knew he had to put on a good show. He was the reason we were all stuck going on this super family vacation. "Like a wonderland."

Quietly, I murmured, "More like creepy." This forest was exactly the sort of place freaks and kidnappers might hide out when they were waiting to attack. Thick underbrush and stinky air would provide the perfect cover for any crime. No one would ever find a body, and hermits could hide out for years without anyone spotting them— big, hairy creeps with axes and wooden sticks, just waiting to attack sweet-smelling city girls.

I shivered. I could think of no worse place to spend a whole month.

Of all the things I *could* be doing in August, living at some broken-down resort on a lake with a bunch of strangers would probably be, oh, let's see . . . my *last* choice. Unfortunately, I didn't get a choice. Even though both of my best friends had offered me a bed at either of their houses for the month, my parents had insisted that I join them. I guess if my mom was being forced to go, I wasn't going to get out of our family adventure. Suffering together is so much more fun.

My parents kept telling me to quit moaning, since it was *just one month*. But I didn't *want* to quit moaning. In this *one* (horrible) *month*, I was going to miss Sylvie's birthday party, the weekend with everyone at Heidi's dad's lake house, and my annual back-to-school shopping with the girls. I was missing everything. I *hate* being left out.

Unless we're talking about this family trip, and then I'd *love* to be left out.

After five torturous hours of driving, we were finally less than ten minutes from Pine Lodge Resort on Lake Whatchamacallit (I hadn't bothered to remember the real name)—and I wasn't feeling any more optimistic about the month ahead.

"Everyone else is arriving today, as well," my dad said, turning his body so he could make eye contact with me in the backseat. My dad was big on eye contact. As an advertising executive, he had a lot of opinions about communication in general. Tone of voice, body language, word choice—apparently, there are rules about all of those things. And I never get the rules right. If you asked my parents, they'd tell you I don't do much of anything right. "We're all going to cook out together tonight. You can get friendly with my coworkers' kids."

"Great," I muttered. "Delightful."

"Your tone says otherwise," said my dad. Unsmiling, he fixed his bright-green eyes—eyes that matched mine exactly, even down to the little brown spots around the pupils—on me. I squirmed and looked away. When my dad was in work mode, which was almost always the last year or so, he kind of freaked me out. Unfortunately, we were going to this lakeside dump with all of his new coworkers, so I had a feeling he was going to be in work mode (a.k.a. downright scary) all month. My dad was so *serious* all the time when he was Mr. Ad Man. Actually, he was pretty serious and Not Fun most of the time lately, so maybe it's not fair to blame work. "Your mother already asked you to change your attitude."

"Consider it changed," I said sweetly, because tone was everything. Dad gave me one of his meaningful looks, then spun back to watch the road ahead.

I slumped in my seat. My puppy, a Vizsla-and-something-else mix that I got from the Humane Society a few weeks ago as a reward for my sixth-grade year-end report card, scrambled into my lap. I rubbed Coco's ears, and she buried her head under my hand. I loved the way her loose puppy skin felt like velvet, warm and comforting. "I'm glad we're in this together," I whispered. Coco whimpered, then let out a low whine, which made me laugh. At least I wasn't the only one complaining.

Moments later, without warning, the paved road ended and the trees spread out a bit. We thumped through potholes, and little rocks kicked up at the underside of our car. My mom guided us along a now narrow, rocky road. Her knuckles were white. She was gripping the steering wheel like it might fall off. I noticed that her fresh manicure was already chipped— my mom and I both had a problem with picking at our nails, but she refused to admit that she had any nervous habits. She carried a little bottle of touch-up polish with her everywhere so no one would ever know.

Up ahead, sunlight glinted off a smallish-looking lake. Out either side of the car there were cabins that looked like something straight out of every horror movie ever made. They had flaking reddish-brown paint and rotting front steps, and it seemed that each one was tinier than the one next to it. "Where are we staying?" I asked. I sat up taller in my seat, craning my neck to try to see what the main lodge looked like.

My mom laughed. It was a brittle and unfamiliar sound.

"It's not funny," I said. Suddenly, Mom pulled the car to the side of the rocky road and turned it off. She continued to chuckle. "Seriously . . ." I was starting to worry. The truth was, my mom only laughed when she'd had a little too much wine, or when she was making fun of someone. "Where's the main lodge? Pine Lodge?"

Now my dad was laughing too. "*Lodge?*" he asked. "We're in the Cardinal cabin—the pine trees that surround us are our natural lodge. We'll be living in nature here at the resort. 'Lodge' is a loose term."

I looked out the car window at the broken-down shacks that surrounded us like prison cells. Coco let out a low whine. I really wanted to join her. If I'd been alone, I would probably have released a sad howl or a whine or a growl—I wasn't sure if I was upset or scared or downright angry.

One of the cabins, the crumbling shack that was closest to our car, had a hand-painted sign that read BLUEJAY. Another, CROW. A third, ROBIN. I was sensing a theme. "We're staying in one of *these*?"

"Of course we're staying in one of these," my mom said, without a hint of apology in her voice. I caught her rolling her eyes in the rearview mirror. And they wonder where I get my attitude! "It's a cottage."

"This? Is not a cottage. It's a bunch of rotten wood that's been piled up in the shape of a tiny cabin. Maybe the owners of this place *wish* it was a cottage, but it would take a lot of fairy dust and dwarf-magic to turn this into something sweet like a cottage. Cottages are for fairy tales and English villages. This is worse than loser Girl Scout camp." I sat and stewed in the backseat, refusing to move. I had expected bad—but this was worse. Sylvie gave me a fresh pedicure for this? So not worth it.

My parents ignored me while they began to unload bags and boxes of food from the back of the car. Every time they glanced my way, I shot them a look of pure evil. I wasn't being unreasonable. I hadn't expected a four-star hotel, like the W. But maybe I'd been thinking this would be something along the lines of a Comfort Suites. Because the thing is, *that* was roughing it. *This* was like some sort of survival show on TV.

Eventually, I opened the door and stepped out onto the rocky ground. Coco followed me, sniffing at piles of this and chunks of that. I didn't even want to think about what my sweet puppy might smell like when she curled up beside me in bed that night.

As I picked my way across the rocky ground, I stuffed my

hands in the pockets of my new black sundress. I didn't want to accidentally touch something disgusting. I'm no diva, but I *am* a city girl. This whole roughing-it business was going to take some getting used to. The air still smelled like cow poop, but now it mixed with the scent of pine and wet grass and old wood. It wasn't actually all *that* bad, but I wasn't going to admit it. I'd already made my point. Now I had to stick by it.

"This way!" my dad called, waving from over by a cabin that was squeezed between two others. Somehow, it looked like it had been neglected at least a hundred years longer than all the others. "I found a Cardinal!"

"Is it dead?" I muttered under my breath. I didn't bother carrying my bag to the cabin. If I left it in the car long enough, one of my parents would bring it inside. They'd nag me and nag me, but I knew if I ignored them, eventually they would just do it themselves. I found that to be true in most situations—if I ignored something long enough, someone else would usually deal with it for me.

I pushed the screen in the cabin's door to open it. But instead of the door springing open, the screen popped out of the door frame. I kicked at the wooden frame, and the door flew open and slammed against the wooden wall inside. "So this is home for the month, eh?"

My dad nodded from just inside the door. He was blocking my path inside our home sweet home, as though he was hiding something. Probably, he'd found a dead mouse or six that he didn't want me to see. Maybe I'd sleep in the car all month. "We can unpack later. I think I heard some people down by the lake. The team isn't starting creative sessions until tomorrow, and I'd like to get some quality relaxing time in with the gang before then."

I have never understood the world of advertising, but I really don't get my dad's new company at all. Just three months ago, he was hired as senior account director at a branding, advertising, and media strategy company called You, Only Better. His firm's offices were in the heart of downtown, in a restored old loft, which was pretty cool. What wasn't cool was the team's annual retreat to the north woods. But You, Only Better had several woodsy sort of clients—an outdoor gear retailer, a bunch of climbing gyms, and a number of organic and natural product companies—that kept their advertising dollars with my dad's company only *because* the firm's creative team went "back to nature" once a year for a month of creative brainstorming and ad development.

"Ready?" Dad asked, eyebrows raised. He began to cross

his arms, then unfolded them again—everyone knew crossed arms sent a bad signal. Something about being closed off and guarded.

I shrugged, crossed my arms, and reluctantly followed him down a path toward the lake. Coco trotted along behind me. We walked over the crest of a pine needle–strewn hill, and I could see a dirty-looking beach area and a rickety dock jutting out into the lake. I squared my shoulders and stood tall. It's easy to fake confidence when you're tall like me.

I was eager to make a strong first impression, until I saw the people I was trying to impress. A group of dorky-looking adults were clustered on and around the dock, drinking sodas and eating chips. *Zit food*, I thought, wondering if they realized how bad that stuff was for their skin.

I scanned the faces that had all turned to look at us. A few people waved and shouted their hellos. My dad waved back, but he isn't a big shouter—he prefers one-on-one greetings and cheesy handshake-hugs. He reminds me of a small-town mayor, the kind of guy who might ride on the back of a convertible in the Fourth of July parade, patting babies and shaking hands. As Dad walked forward to do his thing, my eyes slid over the group of adults wearing ugly shorts and hideous terry-cloth swimsuit cover-ups.

Slowly, I turned my attention to a group of kids who looked about my age. They were sitting on the ground on the rock-and-sand beach. I tried to keep my expression cool as I looked each of them in the eye in turn. It was time to establish my alpha status. But even though I was giving them the look I had perfected for the first day of school, the one my best friend Heidi called the "Isabella Caravelli Scary Smile," no one seemed fazed. I pushed out my lips and narrowed my eyes, the way my mom sometimes does, trying to look a little more threatening.

Suddenly, I sucked in my breath. Two faces in the group were familiar. Too familiar. I swallowed and looked down. I needed a second to collect myself. I wasn't prepared for this.

Once I'd regained my composure, I crossed my arms over my chest and looked up again. Then I smiled straight at them. They obviously recognized me, too. I felt a rush of power as their smiles crumbled.

Chapter Two

Bailey Heath and Ava Young (I was *pretty* sure those were their last names) looked like someone had kicked them in the stomach. Me, presumably. "Hi, Isabella," Bailey said, after a long pause that got more than a little awkward.

"What are you doing here?" I demanded, refusing to tell Bailey to call me "Izzy." Izzy is for friends, and Bailey certainly wasn't that. From what I could tell, Bailey was *weird*, not anything close to a friend of mine. I narrowed my eyes, not bothering to be polite. I was too skeeved out for polite. What were the odds that I'd actually *know* someone at this stupid resort?

As I considered that, I realized the other kids in the group were staring at me. It gave me the willies, the way these strangers were looking at me like I was some sort of freak. The whole scene made me the tiniest bit uncomfortable, since I was totally out of my comfort zone. Neither of my best friends was by my side, my parents were on edge, and I was being stared at. Not in a good way. Without thinking, I began to pick at my pinkie fingernail, but I caught myself before I could do much damage. I crossed my arms again instead.

After another long pause, Ava laughed, an awkward snort. She had the kind of laugh that makes you feel bad for her. I turned to look at her, watching as she nervously fiddled with the rocks at her side, letting her thin blond hair hang over her eyes. "We live here," Ava said with a shrug, pushing her hair away from her face. Then she blushed. "I mean, in August we live here. At the lake. Obviously not the rest of the year. Since we go to school with you. So . . ." Ava trailed off, and I smirked. It made me feel better, somehow, seeing how flustered Ava got while she was talking to me.

The thing is, that almost always happens when people like Ava talk to me. I don't know how or when it happened, but for as long as I can remember, I've made people a little— sometimes a lot—nervous. My best friend Sylvie thinks its because I'm more beautiful than everyone else in our grade. I guess I don't really see that. I can understand why some people might think I'm pretty—even adults seem to envy my long, straight black hair—but hair really isn't everything, and there are lots of people who are gorgeous at our school. Most of them don't have my ugly knees or two ears that stick out if they don't put their hair *just so*. Obviously, I don't *talk* about my knees or my ears, and no one seems to have noticed them yet.

My other best friend, Heidi, says people act differently around me because I have a super-stubborn personality and don't take crap from anyone. I don't really know what that means—I mean, I guess I try not to let people get to me. It doesn't always work, but I usually put on a pretty good show. I learned from my mom that if you don't let people see your ruffled feathers, they'll never even know they're there. It's all about the polish.

Even though I don't really get why people act this way around me, I do like it. It's fun, watching people crumble when I look at them a certain way. The thing is, if people want to feel threatened by me, that's their choice. I always treat other people the way they expect to be treated—and sometimes people expect me to be sort of horrible to them. So sue me if I'm the girl a lot of people don't like. Maybe my friends and I had sometimes made Bailey and Ava's first year of middle school somewhat . . . difficult. But the thing is, there's a certain order in school, and I just happened to be toward the top of the list.

Bailey and Ava, on the other hand, were at the bottom. All three of us knew it. That's why the situation we found ourselves in was so awkward.

"So . . . ," I said, glancing out at the lake. I was trying to pretend I didn't notice the way everyone was just staring at me, as though *I* was some sort of outsider. I suddenly felt like a total freak, and it was seriously bugging me. I didn't look at anyone when I asked, "What do you all do for fun around here?"

I caught Bailey looking at the other kids sitting on the ground next to her, as if she needed someone to tell her what to say. It was a moment of weakness, and I pounced. I raised my eyebrows, looked right at her, and demanded, "So?"

"Swim, canoe, hang out. You know." Bailey grinned and crossed her legs. They were covered in bug bites. I cringed. *This place just keeps getting better.*

"All day? That's what you do all day?" Coco stepped away from my side and sniffed at one of the guys sitting near me. I looked at the guy closely for the first time. *Totally cute!* He had dark-brown eyes, skin that was somewhere between a caramel and cocoa color, and cool lobster-print board shorts. His hair was all messed up, like he'd pushed it away from his face when he finished swimming, then let it dry that way. My hair never did anything fun like that, it just sort of lay there, all perfect and unruffled.

This guy looked like he was a little older than me— eighth grade, maybe. I'd have to find out. The guys going into seventh grade at our school are all so immature. It would be cool to hang out with someone older, for once. And I obviously had to find someone other than Bailey and Ava to hang out with at the lake, since they were totally boring. I peeked at his board shorts again, and silently nicknamed him Lobster Boy.

Cutie-pie Lobster Boy smiled up at me, and I felt my stomach twist. I shot my cutest smile back at him—*now* it was worth being polite!—just as he said, "Yes, that is what we do *all day.*"

It wasn't *what* he said but the *way* he said it. . . . I knew he was mocking me. Lobster Boy rubbed at the soft skin on the underside of Coco's neck and turned to grin at the others in the group of misfits.

"Oh," I said simply. I tried to stay calm, but I felt my voice catch when I saw Bailey and Ava exchanging a look. Suddenly it felt like they were all ganging up on me. It was as though I'd been dumped into some sort of alternate universe where no one understood that *I* was the only one who could talk to people the way Lobster Boy had just talked to me. I snapped to get Coco's attention. My puppy had snuggled up against the hot guy who was mocking me. *Traitor,* I thought, scowling at my dog. "Well, have fun with that. See you around."

As I began to walk away, Ava called out, "Hey, Isabella?"

I turned. Ava had stood up as if she were going to come after me. Suddenly, I felt a little bit better. Maybe I'd just gotten off to a bad start. They obviously didn't know me yet, and most of them didn't know how things usually went in this sort of situation. "Yeah, Bailey?"

Ava cringed. "Um, I'm Ava?"

"Oh," I said, crossing my arms again. "Sorry!" I smiled, trying to make it seem like the name mix-up was just an innocent mistake.

"You should change into your suit and come hang out with us." Ava curled her toes into the sand at her feet.

I continued to smile, my polite smile that I usually reserved for teachers and my parents' most generous friends. I considered it for a second. But I didn't want to seem too eager. I knew I needed to show the other kids that I have plenty of other things to do without following them around. "No, thanks. But you guys have fun, okay?"

As I walked off, someone quietly asked, "You know her?"

Ava and Bailey both muttered, "Yes." I knew they were probably going to talk about me as soon as I was out of earshot. *Whatever.*

I reached down to pat Coco. She looked up at me with her warm chocolate eyes and I bent over to pick her up. I snuggled my face into her soft fur and tried to convince myself that it was no big deal. People talked about me all the time, but it's not like it ever mattered. Mostly, people were just jealous. Right? That's what I always told myself—and Heidi and Sylvie always agreed—but I sometimes wondered if it was true.

As I carried Coco back up the hill to our creepy little cabin, I couldn't stop myself from worrying about what Bailey and Ava might be saying. My stomach was churning with nerves, the way it did before choir solos and math tests. Because the thing is, there were a few teensy things that I had been a part of last year that Bailey and Ava would certainly blab about to the others. Things that probably sounded sort of mean, if you told the story a certain way.

I'd had my share of fun during our first year at Southwest Middle School—mostly just pranks and games, but sometimes people got so sensitive about stuff. Like the time Heidi and I stole some girls' clothes from the locker room during swimming unit in gym. It was hilarious watching five flat-chested sixth graders streaking through the hall to the office in nothing but swimsuits . . . but I suddenly had a feeling Ava and Bailey and their other friends might not have seen the humor in it.

And then there was spirit day, when everyone sent flowers to their friends and boyfriends and stuff. Sylvie and I bought thirty red carnations, then sent them—with fake notes and these horrible, goopy love poems—to all of the most popular eighth-grade guys. The notes were all different, but there were two that I was particularly proud of. One, which I'd paired with a really lame sonnet, said, "I'll love you always and forever, through the test of time . . . Bailey Heath." The other, which we sent with a goofy and babyish version of "Roses Are Red," was signed "Secretly yours forever, Ava Young." I grinned, thinking about how the girls who had supposedly sent the flowers had been mercilessly teased by the entire soccer team—and my friends and me— for weeks.

It's not my fault that no one ever tries to get me back. Anyone can pull pranks, but no one else ever does it. And now, I was sure that Ava and Bailey were probably whining about me.

It's not like I wanted to be buddy-buddy with the other random kids who were dragged along on their parents' work trips, but I also didn't have any other friends here. And August was a long month to spend on my own.

For the first time in a very long while, I felt the tiniest bit lonely.

Chapter Three

~~~~~~~~~~~~~~~~

Before I got even halfway back up the path to our ramshackle Cardinal cabin, I turned and marched back down the hill.

People have no right to talk about me without me being a part of it. I don't like not knowing what's being said. If they were going to talk about me, I had a right to listen. I needed the ammo to retaliate.

I stepped off the main path, squeezing between a grove of newly planted trees and a huge, hollowed-out one that looked like it had fallen and been left to rot at least half a century ago. The log was teeming with insects and covered in moss. It was the sort of place raccoons might hide out during the day, before they came out to hunt twelve-going-on-thirteen-year-olds at night.

I shivered. The idea of rabid raccoons gave me the creeps, so I hustled through the brush. I carefully picked my way over stumps and around a pile of tiny little animal pellets—*ew!*—until I could hear voices and see the lake shining through the trees ahead. Let me just clarify now that the lake had a *dull* shine. This was not a body of water that deserved its own postcard or even an ugly amateur photograph in some hoity-toity local art gallery. I don't even think our school librarian would consider this a lake that would be worthy of her odd collection of photo coffee mugs. It was full of weeds and had a sort of green sheen to it that made it look like it was possibly full of disease. It probably was.

Coco squirmed in my arms, whining to get down. I kissed her fuzzy ears and whispered, "Promise you won't bark and give me away?" Coco looked at me, then licked my nose. It surprised me enough that I giggled. "That's good enough. I trust you." I set her on the ground and continued to walk, slowly, toward the beach.

I could hear my dad's loud laugh echoing toward me from the dock, and my shoulders slumped. Dad never laughed like that with me anymore. He never had time to do anything fun anymore, and he hardly ever joked around the way he used to—at least, not with me. With his coworkers and his "team," he always pretended to be this easygoing Mr. Cool Guy. At home, though, Dad's stressed out all the time. It annoys me that strangers get to see the fun side of Dad that he used to save for me—even if it's all for show. In some ways, Mom's (not-so-secret) stranger anxiety is better than the way my dad acts. At least she's not being fakey with people.

As I picked my way through scratchy bushes and thick piles of dead leaves—*ow!*—I crouched down low so none of the kids gathered on the beach could see me. After a few more shaky steps, I sat down on a low rock that made a perfect snooping stool. I listened closely for Bailey's loud, gasping laugh or Ava's squeaky voice. I knew I had to be close.

Coco crawled onto my lap, and her eyes drifted closed. Her little body shuddered, then she sighed and fell fast asleep. "It's like you haven't been sleeping for the last five hours," I whispered.

Suddenly, the sound of girls' laughter put me on high alert. I couldn't see them, but I knew Ava and Bailey and the others were less than ten feet away from me, just on the other side of a thick mess of wild blueberry bushes.

I held my breath, suddenly worried I'd be caught. It wouldn't look good if they found me hunched over here, crawling through brambles. I could say I lost a headband?

Needed wood for . . . ? Oh! I'm hunting for blueberries! I knew I could come up with something if I needed to, and at the moment, all I could think about was how much I *needed* to know what Ava and Bailey were going to say about me. Knowledge is power, my dad always says, and in the case of gossip it's always the truth. I was sort of the master at figuring out how to use people's words against them, and I intended to do just that. If necessary, of course.

"Impossible," someone said. The voice sounded like the cute guy, the one who'd made fun of me! Lobster Boy. "She didn't do that."

"Not a lie," Bailey said, laughing her donkey laugh again. If only she could figure out how to close her mouth before she took a breath, she wouldn't sound like a farm animal. "Pinkie swear."

Pinkie swear? I rolled my eyes. What was she, six?

Bailey continued. "I was there. Really! It happened."

They *were* talking about me! I was sure of it. I grinned, realizing that it was pretty cool that Lobster Boy sounded so impressed. Maybe he'd be worth my time after all.

"Prove it," Lobster Boy said. I heard a shuffling sound, and suddenly his messy hair was bobbing above the brush line just a few feet away—he'd stood up! If he turned around,

I'd be caught snooping, for sure. I tried to slink down, burying myself deeper in the brush, but Coco stirred on my lap when I moved. So I stayed as still as I could and hoped no one would see me lurking in the bushes. What if they thought I was hiding back here, peeing in the woods or something? Oh, the humiliation.

Suddenly, Bailey stood up right beside Lobster Boy. I wondered what she was going to show him to prove what I'd done. . . . Was she going to try to demonstrate how I'd stolen their swimsuits? Or maybe she'd recite one of the poems? Oh! This was getting better and better. I loved hearing how other people told stories about me.

Before I could wonder any more, Ava leapt up and ran into the water. She jogged out until the water was about thigh-deep, then dove under. Everyone else stood up to watch her. Bailey reached down and grabbed a little Flip video camera, pointing it in the direction of whatever was going on in the lake. I had to crane my neck to try to see what was happening, which was tricky since there was this huge branch in the way. After almost half a minute had passed, Ava resurfaced right by a buoy that was way out in the lake.

"Told ya!" Bailey cried. She jumped up and down with her camera, cheering for Ava. "Woo-hoo!"

"That is seriously impossible," Lobster Boy called loudly. "I'm impressed."

Impressed by a girl who can hold her breath and swim for twenty whole seconds? *What?* If I'd done something that lame with my friends, they would have laughed so hard Heidi would be crying. Apparently, though, Lobster Boy was easily impressed. Maybe he wasn't quite as cute as I'd been giving him credit for.

That's when I realized that they maybe *hadn't* been talking about me at all. . . . Was it possible that they'd been talking about Ava's stupid water tricks the whole time? When were they going to talk about me? Surely, they were *going* to talk about me.

But I listened for a while longer, waiting to hear my name. Still nothing. All they talked about was their "amazing" swimming challenges, and about something dorky called Canoe Wars. Finally, I realized I was eavesdropping on the most boring conversation in the history of time. Okay, maybe that was sort of exaggerating—but this was definitely close to the most boring conversation ever. It was the most boring conversation *I'd* ever heard. So how lame did it make me that I was actually *listening* to it? That I'd climbed over animal poo (excrement!) to listen to it?

I stood up, holding Coco tightly so she wouldn't squirm as I escaped my hiding spot. I picked my way over branches and past the dead tree, walking faster and faster until I was back at my so-called cottage again. What a waste of time! Annoyed, I kicked at the bottom of the door and watched as it rattled. I felt foolish for wasting my time snooping on people who obviously had nothing interesting to talk about. What if I'd been caught? I shuddered at the thought that *these* people might judge me, then pushed open the door to the cabin and stormed inside.

I hadn't gotten a good look at the Cardinal cabin when we first arrived, because my dad had been so busy hustling me down to the lake to make first impressions. I should have just stayed back, since my first impression didn't go at all the way I would have liked. As Coco found her bed in the corner by the door, I scanned the dimly lit room. The living room was separated from the kitchen by a wall of low-hanging cabinets. Someone had scratched something totally inappropriate onto the back of one of the cabinets. Another someone had made the bad choice to paint over the scratching . . . which made it look like the crude word was an unframed work of art hanging on the living room side of the cabinet wall.

All the walls and furniture in the tiny cabin were wood,

which made it seem a little more cottage-like. But the whole place also just looked uncomfortable, like I was going to get splinters in my butt every time I sat down to look through a magazine. There was nowhere to flop—I would have happily traded Lobster Boy for my fluffy rug from home—and nowhere to curl up. I had a feeling I'd be spending a lot of time alone, planted in one of these splintery seats, unless some miracle happened and I suddenly wanted to hang out with two of the biggest nobodies from my school. And it wasn't like that was going to happen. Even if they came crawling back to beg me to hang out with them.

I peeked into the bathroom, which was small and rustic (meaning "old"). The sink was so tiny I could hardly fit both hands inside the basin, and the toilet had a crack in the seat that looked like it would pinch. There was no point in even looking at the shower, since the shower curtain was old and musty, so I could only imagine what the shower itself might look like. I was probably going to get foot fungus.

There were two bedrooms—thank goodness. As I'd suspected might happen, my bag had found its way from the car to my room, and my clothes had already been unpacked and neatly folded in the dresser drawers. This was my mother's specialty. Sara Hurst-Caravelli (a.k.a. my delightful mother) had a certain way of doing everything, and I was much better off if I just stayed out of her way. If I'd unpacked for myself, I would have been forced to redo it. But if my mom just did things for me in the first place, she had less reason to be critical of how these things were done. That way, we were all winners.

I could hear my mom talking on her cell phone in my parents' room, which was just next door. The walls between the bedrooms were thin and the door was a wispy fabric curtain, so I could easily hear snippets of conversation. My mom's business wasn't all that interesting—she was probably just talking to one of my aunts, who seemed to be her only real friends these days—so I pulled my own phone out of my bag and checked for new texts.

Nothing.

How could there be nothing? Maybe there wasn't any service at the lake? Nope, three bars.

I quickly dashed off a short text to Heidi, then sent one to Sylvie. Neither one of them wrote back instantly, which was what I'd really wanted. I wanted my best friends to miss me, and I wanted someone to be thinking of me. But more than anything, I didn't want to be at a broken-down "cottage" with my griping parents and a bunch of nobodies and two freaks

from my middle school when I could have been somewhere—
anywhere—else.

After quickly checking for rogue mice who might be hiding under the pillows, I flounced down on my bed. I stared
up at the ceiling, which I noticed was also made of wood
(was *everything* made of wood?), and wondered what I was
supposed to do next. I flopped from my back to my front,
trying to get comfortable on the sagging mattress. My mother
had made my bed for me, and I felt a little more comfortable
because at least the blanket was from home.

As I tried not to listen to the sound of my mom laughing
on the phone in the next room, I picked at my fingernails.
One began to bleed.

Coco pattered into the bedroom and launched herself onto
the bed beside me. "What do we do now?" I asked quietly,
stroking my dog's smushy body. Coco just stared back. It turns
out, dogs are great for hugs but not as great for company.

"Isabella?" My mom broke through the silence from the
room next door.

"What?"

She sighed loudly enough for me to hear it through both
of our curtained doors. "Why aren't you down at the lake
with the other kids?"

"I could ask you the same question."

"Don't be like that," she ordered.

"Why aren't I there?" I said, trying to keep my voice pleasant. "Because I'm in here."

The mattress in the other room groaned as she stood up and walked into my room. She squinted at me, as though the very sight of me gave her a headache. "But *why* are you here?"

"Why are *you* here? There's a dock full of adults down there, just waiting to be charmed." We both knew that she didn't like strangers. Her best friends are her two sisters, and they can probably only stand her because they live hundreds of miles away. The thing about my mom is, she's usually sort of friendly to other adults at school events, or at holiday parties with their regular group of acquaintances—but a month with mostly strangers in a foreign land was probably going to make her go slowly insane. She hated making nice with people who didn't matter. (She also hated when I said stuff like that, but it was the truth and we both knew it.)

Luckily, Mom had picked up two consulting projects that were due at the end of the month. So that would give her a good excuse to hang out inside and work more than was necessary. I knew Dad had forced my mom to come to the lake—I'd heard them arguing about it plenty of times—probably because it would look bad if he came alone. My dad was all about appearances, and if everyone else's family was joining them at the lake, then he would make sure *his* family would be at the lake too.

My mom put her hand on her hip. I could tell she was annoyed with me, since she breathed in and out twice. *Inhale. Exhale. Inhale. Exhale.* "That's your father's job."

"Well, there you go, then," I said simply. "You said it yourself. It's *Dad's* job to be down there, mingling. It's *my* job to sit up here and try to take part in the summer you dragged me away from back home." I smiled and waved my phone in the air. "I'm going to participate in my real life via text, so it will almost be like I'm at home with my real friends." I looked her straight in the eye and smiled. "Fun summer, huh?"

She stared back, stone-faced. Then she studied me carefully. "Are you picking your nails again?" she asked. "Why do you do that? Can't you just leave well enough alone?"

"I like my bloody stumps, thanks." I started to wiggle my fingers in the air, taunting. But then I realized I'd already pushed my limit, so I quickly stuffed my hands under my body to try to prevent any further conversation about them. "You know it's a habit."

"Well, break it," she demanded, then stormed out of the

room. She banged around in the kitchen for a while, while I stared at the blank screen on my phone.

Through the open window in my bedroom, I could hear the sounds of people gathering in the common outdoor area in the center of all the cabins. I'd forgotten about the get-to-know-you barbecue. Now I was stuck making a choice: Stay inside with one critical, crabby, and stranger-anxious mom, or brave the group of misfits again and see if there was anyone worth my time. I heard the ding of the tiny microwave—Lean Cuisine dinner!—and knew it was an easy choice.

When my mom was nuking broccoli, things were about to start to stink.

Chapter Four

Outside, a campfire was already roaring and several barbecues had been loaded with charcoal. There were probably about thirty people altogether, enough that I should have been able to hide and observe for a while before I'd have to find someone to talk to. But instead of me getting to stand back, coolly watching, my dad spotted me and ruined everything. As soon as he saw me, he called me over to where he stood with a group of people who were all wearing socks and sandals.

"Isabella, I'd like you to meet Chuck and Craig, who run the design team." Two dudes, both in plaid shorts, said hello. One of them—Chuck? It really didn't matter—had a piece of lettuce or something stuck in his teeth, and no one had been nice enough to give him a heads-up. I thought about saying something, but my dad spoke again before I got the chance. "And this is John, who does our media strategy." John winked, and I did my best to smile back. John seemed like a creep. "Of course, you already know Erica Winter, the big boss." My dad laughed, and Erica the Big Boss joined him even though it wasn't the least bit funny. The whole scene was disturbing. Erica should have been offended that someone called her Big, when she was anything but, but it didn't seem to bother her.

"Nice to meet you all," I said, understanding that my job was to smile and pretend to be the great daughter my dad wished he had. "Good to see you again, Ms. Winter."

"It's Erica," she said. "No need for formality at the lake."

"Right," I said, nodding and smiling like a puppet. I watched as my mom picked her way down the cabin stairs, her smile forced. She strolled up to stand beside my dad and greeted the other adults. It was always so embarrassing, watching my mom with adults she didn't know—she smiled really awkwardly, and said, "So . . ." a lot to make up for any lulls in the conversation.

"Have you met the other kids?" John said, winking at me again. I began to wonder if perhaps John had some sort of condition—a medical problem that made him wink way too much, rather than just a creepy middle-aged-man winking issue. "Chuck's daughter Ava is about your age." He turned and pointed to where Ava stood with Bailey and Lobster Boy and three other people I recognized from down at the beach.

Erica added, "My daughter Bailey mentioned that you go to Southwest too? I'm surprised none of us put two and two together that you'd all be spending the summer up here together."

"It's a big school," I said, because it was the truth. There are almost three hundred kids in my class alone. Three different elementary schools in the district feed into Southwest Middle School, where we all get mixed together into one big class of sixth graders. We'll all be stuck together until we graduate, which is part of the reason I worked so hard in sixth grade to establish myself as someone important. It's easy to become a nobody when middle school starts. Nobodies have no control at all, and how horrible would that be? I could think of nothing worse. "We haven't had any classes together, so I don't really know Bailey very well." I tried to sound vague. I wondered if Bailey had told her mom about the swimsuit-stealing thing or the spirit-day poems? Probably. People like Bailey always told.

"Well, it will be fun for you all to spend some time

together this month," Erica said with a smile. "Get to know some more people from your class."

I shrugged, and my mom said, "So . . ."

I could feel my father giving me a look. "Yeah," I said politely, and crossed my arms. I knew I had to at least try to be decent to my dad's boss. "It will be nice to get to know them. Hey, Dad, do we have any soda?"

"Help yourself to anything you can find around here," Erica offered. "Bailey can get you something out of our cooler if you haven't had time to get your things unpacked yet."

"Okay," I said. "Thanks." I took that as my cue to leave. I could feel the adults watching me, so I reluctantly wandered over toward where the rest of the kids sat near the bonfire. One little kid, who looked about ten, was throwing beetles into the fire and he screeched every time one popped.

Bailey and Ava both waved as I walked toward them. I figured it couldn't hurt to be nice, so I waved back. "Hey, Bailey," I said. "Your mom said I could steal a soda from your cooler?"

"Oh!" Bailey said. "Yeah! Sure! I'll get you one! Caffeine or not?"

"Surprise me." I watched as Bailey hustled off, hurrying to get me my drink. It almost seemed like she thought it was some sort of honor to get me a soda. While I waited, I sat down on one of the logs beside the fire pit. Little bits of bark poked through my dress, and I realized I was probably going to have to wear jeans from now on. Both for protection and to avoid the bugs. I certainly didn't want legs that looked like Bailey's or Ava's—all chewed up and nasty.

To avoid having to talk to anyone, I studied my hands. I was glad I'd packed a set of fake nails in my bag. I'd already done a number on my real nails in just a few hours at the lake. I curled my hands into balls and tried not to think about how gross they looked. Could other people see them? I hoped not. I didn't mean to pick at my fingernails, but when I got nervous, I just couldn't help it.

Tomorrow, my nerves would be gone. By tomorrow, I would figure out how to make sure things went my way. And then I could cover up my ugly nails and fix everything.

Bailey jogged up and thrust a can of Cherry Coke in my face. "I hope cherry's okay?"

I shrugged. "It's fine." Bailey stood there, waiting for something. I didn't know what. I squinted at her and asked, "Do you want me to give you some money for the Coke?"

"Oh," Bailey said, her blue eyes wide. That's when I noticed for the first time that Bailey was really pretty. Her hair was curly and long, and this really cool copper color. She had tiny freckles that dotted her cheeks, the kind I'd always wanted. She looked a little like the American Girl doll that I'd loved when I was little. But unlike my doll, who always had on the cutest clothes, Bailey was dressed in ripped shorts and a too-big T-shirt. Also, her hair was sort of crazy and flyaway, like she'd been shoved in the back of someone's closet for too long. That video camera I'd seen her with earlier was stuffed in her back pocket, which made it look like she had some sort of unfortunate growth on her butt. "No, of course you don't have to give me money." After a pause, she quietly added, "You're welcome."

The other kids in the group were looking at me funny. That's when I realized I had forgotten to say thank you. I knew it was rude to say nothing when she'd gone and fetched me a soda, but I really did just forget. It wasn't an intentional diss. But I also knew that if I caved and said thanks now, after Bailey had prompted me, I would look pitiful. So instead, I just popped open the top of my soda and took a big swallow.

"I'm Brennan," Lobster Boy said suddenly. So suddenly that I choked on my soda a little bit. "And this is my brother, Zach." He pointed at the bug-roasting kid, who was wearing nothing but a pair of swim trunks. "In case you were wondering."

"Isabella," I said in response. "It's nice to meet you."

"This is my little sister, Madeline," Ava said quietly. "She's ten. I know she looks older than me." Ava blushed. Even though she was younger than her sister, Madeline was at least as tall as Ava. Ava was short and wiry, while Madeline was tall and strong-looking. The only thing that made them look like sisters was their matching white-blond hair.

"And that guy over there, the one getting sticks for marshmallows, is Levi," Brennan said. "He likes to whittle."

"Whistle?" I asked, wondering if Brennan had a lisp.

"Whittle," Lobster Boy Brennan said slowly, as though I was stupid. "Wood."

I shrugged, still confused. "Oh." I felt all their eyes on me, as though I was supposed to say something more. As if everyone in the world had heard of whittling, and I was some sort of weirdo for being clueless. They all continued to stare. It felt like minutes passed, but it was probably only about two seconds. Still, I'd never been in this position before—where people were expecting me to say something, but I had nothing at all to say. It almost felt like they were auditioning me for the role of "Friend" in a TV movie or something. But I'm not the kind of girl who auditions. People just *want* to be my friend. That's the way it's always worked, for as long as I could remember.

But even as I tried to convince myself of that, I kept getting more and more nervous. It was obvious that Brennan, Zach, Bailey, Ava, Madeline, and Levi all knew each other. Knew each other *well*, in fact. I was the outsider. "What's whittling?" I asked finally, just to get them to stop staring. Maybe someone would say something and break the uncomfortable silence. My pinkie fingernail had started to bleed again, and I hadn't even realized I was picking at it. I tucked it against my palm, hoping no one would see.

"Whittling," Levi said from behind me, "is this." He poked me in the back with some sort of stick that he'd shaved into a fine point with a small knife. "Want to try?"

"I don't think so," I said, setting my soda down on the ground. I suddenly felt sick. It was like I was in some sort of parallel universe. Who were these people? Just as Levi poked me in the back again, I felt my phone vibrate in my pocket. Saved by a text from Heidi: "Miss u like crazy! Bored yet?"

I quickly sent one back that said: "This place is full of freaks." Then I smiled to myself, feeling better to have the comment out of my body. I was an outsider here, but so what?

These people *were* freaks. I didn't need to be a part of their little club. I had no interest in whittling, I certainly wasn't going to roast bugs in a fire, and I already knew I wasn't going to be best friends with Ava or Bailey. What was the point in even faking my way through one night?

When I looked up from my phone to see what they'd ask me next, I realized that everyone's attention had shifted while I'd been on my phone. They were talking about something else, and no one cared that I was back to rejoin the conversation. I sat there for a while longer, sipping my soda and waiting for another text, until eventually I slipped away from the bonfire and went back to my cabin.

The only thing that bugged me? When I looked back, I realized none of them had even noticed I was gone.

Chapter Five

~~~~~~~~~~~~~~~~~~~~

For the next couple of days, I kept to myself. Each morning I ate my yogurt and granola on the wooden couch, enjoying a few minutes alone while my parents went out for a walk. It was one of the only times of the day when my mom left the cabin—she always made excuses about staying out of the sun in the middle of the day, and at night she only joined the other adults for a short while before she excused herself because of the bugs.

When she finally did leave the cabin for even a short while, her absence was obvious. The pressure inside the belly of our little Cardinal went *whoosh* the moment she walked out the door. After breakfast, I made a habit of watching out the window as Ava and Bailey and the others traipsed down to the lake. The rest of the day, I lay in my bed and read, stopping only for food and to respond to texts from my friends.

Whenever my dad stopped by the cabin during his team's brainstorming breaks, he gave me these weird meaningful looks, which I pointedly ignored. "The other kids are doing games night tonight," he'd say hopefully. I didn't even bother answering, since I'd found if I ignored him long enough he usually went away. Meanwhile, my mom cleared her throat every time I pulled out my phone, but she never actually said anything to me. So I ignored their looks and throat clearing, and just tried to stay out of the way.

At lunch, Mom would offer to nuke me a Lean Cuisine meal, reminding me each time that it's never too soon to think about calorie control. I'd pass and slurp up a bowl of pasta with pesto or a peanut butter sandwich instead. I knew the fat-filled meals weren't doing me any favors with health-kick Sara, but at least my lunches tasted like real food.

But after two days of the same boring routine, I got antsy. The cabin was way too small for my mom and me to sit and stew in all day, and it was muggy and hot. So late in the afternoon of our third day at the resort, I decided to sneak down to the lake for a quick swim. I strategically waited until most of the adults were working in someone's cabin and the other kids were all out canoeing. I didn't want to have to talk to anyone.

I plodded down to the lake in my swimsuit and waded into the water. I was surprised to find it was cool and refreshing, and you didn't really notice the greenish color when you were up close to the water. I floated for a while, pretending I was in a Caribbean pool, then returned to my cabin to hole away. But the next day, I snuck down to the lake in the afternoon again, just as everyone else was heading back up the hill for a barbecue.

"Hey, Isabella!" Bailey said, rushing over. "What have you been doing all day? You can totally join us for some s'mores in a little bit."

I loved s'mores. But did I love s'mores more than I loved my reputation? "No, thanks." I felt just the tiniest bit bad for saying no, since Bailey and Ava both seemed so desperate to spend time with me.

On the morning of our fifth full day at the lake, I realized I'd moved beyond bored. My mom had started calling me sullen, the inside of our cabin smelled like rotten broccoli and chicken, and I was out of books to read. So I slipped on my pink swimsuit and headed to the lake right after Brennan made his way down the path.

I'd been watching Brennan over the past few days, and decided he was definitely cute. He was certainly worth leaving the cabin for. I dropped my towel on the beach, then waded slowly out into the swimming area. Once my body was used to the cool water, I dove under. When I popped up to the surface again, I rolled over on my back and looked toward shore to see who was watching me.

No one!

I stared at Brennan, willing him to notice me, but he was busy with Ava and Madeline.

I did a handstand underwater, then checked to see who'd noticed *that*.

Not a single person had even glanced my way.

I tried swimming underwater, out to the buoy that had gotten Ava so much attention on our first day at the lake. I dove deep and pulled through the water with my arms, hoping someone was watching. But instead of making it there, I only made it about halfway and then I had to pop out of the water gasping for air. I took a breath too soon and choked on a huge mouthful of water. A weed wrapped around my sticky-outey ear, and I suddenly sounded like I was suffering from whooping cough.

Finally, someone noticed.

"You okay?" Brennan called, shielding his eyes from the sun on the beach.

I spluttered and coughed again.

"Do you need a hand?" he yelled.

I waved my hand, as if to say no, but he must have taken it as a sign that I was drowning or something. Suddenly, he came splashing out into the water toward me, carrying a toddler-size Disney Princess life jacket under his arm. Cinderella and Snow White looked like they were dancing together in the same floaty scene. "I'm fine," I finally managed to choke out.

Brennan stopped short. After a moment, he threw the life jacket at me and ordered, "You should probably wear that while you're out there alone. Just in case."

Fabulous. Just what I need. A baby life jacket. I swam back to shore, dropped the life jacket on the dock, and hustled back up to my cabin. How humiliating!

As soon as I stepped inside the cabin, my mom pounced. "Why are you hunched over like that?" She glanced up from the kitchen table, where her papers were stacked around her in perfectly organized piles.

"Like what?" I asked, straightening.

"You're all slouched." She studied me carefully, letting her eyes travel from the tip of my head to my toes. It was almost as though she'd been sitting there for hours, just waiting for someone to pick on. Guess who that lucky someone was? "Have you gotten any exercise at all since we've arrived?"

"Nope."

"'Nope' is not a word," she reminded me. "Maybe you should get out for a walk or something?"

"I'm happy inside," I lied, through clenched teeth. "Delighted, in fact. Ecstatic. Overjoyed." I hoped I was using enough excellent vocabulary that my mom would just let me pass through.

"You don't look happy *or* ecstatic. You're scowling."

I snapped. "Because you're picking on me! Wouldn't you scowl if you were being attacked?"

"I'm not attacking," she explained in a condescending voice. "I'm helping."

"Well, your helping isn't helping!" I threw my towel in a wet heap on the floor and hustled to my room. I hated feeling like *I* was the weirdo every time I was around the other kids on this horrible work trip, and my mom wasn't making me feel better at all. I didn't get why she had to pick all the time. Why couldn't she just let me be? And where was my dad when I needed someone to stick up for me? With Chuck and Craig and creepy John, that's where.

As a kid, when I was sad, my dad and mom seemed to understand when I just needed a hug . . . but now, the moment either one of them sensed weakness, they attacked me. It wasn't fair.

I picked up my phone and silently pleaded for new messages from my friends. But there was nothing. I hadn't heard from Heidi or Sylvie in over two hours. I sat down on top of my perfectly made bed in my wet swimsuit and stared up at the ceiling, fuming.

When my mom peeked into my room, I quickly picked up my cell and pretended I was doing something important. I opened the TMZ app. Which was important. Sort of.

"Your phone is becoming a problem," Mom said quietly from the curtained doorway.

"How?" I asked, refusing to look at her. She didn't deserve a proper conversation, with eye contact and everything. I could tell when my mom was just picking on me for the sake of picking on something. After almost thirteen years, I knew her well enough to know she had to be at least as bored as I was. She had already reorganized the contents of the kitchen cabinets in our cabin. She'd ironed all of her clothes—twice. I knew *I* was the only project my mother had left, and I wasn't looking forward to the three weeks we had left to just look at each other inside our tiny little "cottage."

She took a deep breath, then said, "I think maybe I need to take your phone so you can actually get out there and enjoy yourself this month."

"Enjoy myself?" I snorted. "As if. The other kids at this place are freaks who act like babies, and the lake smells like manure, and there's nothing fun to do!"

"There's plenty to do."

"Really, Mom? So what have you been doing to take advantage of this fun family vacation spot? Sitting inside with the iron and your laptop?"

"What I do is none of your business. What *you* do, however, *is* my business."

I laughed out loud. It almost sounded like one of Ava's snorts. "Right."

"Hand over the phone," she ordered.

"Not a chance."

"Give me the phone, and I'll return it to you at the end of the month. If you put up a fight now, I'll flat-out cancel your service, and you can wait until you can afford to buy a phone for yourself." She raised her eyebrows, challenging me to find a smart retort. "Your choice."

"Are you kidding me?" I said, suddenly realizing she

was serious. She was trying to take away my only lifeline to home, to normal people, to my friends. If she stole my phone, all I'd have left was Coco. My puppy was adorable, but she was happy doing three things, over and over, all day every day: running, sleeping, and licking her own butt. She wasn't exactly the best conversationalist. "You wouldn't do that to me. It's like I'm a hostage or something."

"I would, and I am." She held out her hand. "Your father and I discussed the situation last night, and now I'm making the executive decision that it's time for you to give it up. And don't think, even for a moment, that you've got things bad. All you've done since we arrived at the lake is lie in your room, hugging your phone. I want to see you outside, doing kid things, instead of being stuck in here acting like a brat."

"I'm not a kid, so don't expect me to be out there playing hopscotch and popping bugs. Besides, you're the one acting like a brat." I regretted my words the moment they crossed my lips. Talking back was one thing, but calling my mother names was another thing altogether. "I didn't mean that," I said. I chewed at my lip, wishing that was enough to distract my mom from processing what I'd just said. I just didn't think it was fair that she was allowed to hide out in the cabin, and I wasn't.

"Your phone," she said calmly, holding out her hand. "Which is, technically, *my* phone. And as we've already discussed, you also have no right to comment on what I am or am not doing. I'm your mother, and what I say goes."

I opened my mouth, then closed it again. Surely, she was just having a bad day. She couldn't really take my phone—the phone I'd just gotten that spring, after months of begging and promising—away from me for the rest of the summer. Could she?

"And how many times do I have to tell you to stop picking at your nails!" she said, sounding all frantic. I looked down and realized I'd been absentmindedly picking at my *other* pinkie nail for who knows how long.

Before I could stop myself, I began to cry. Not the loud, messy kind of tears I used to conjure up to get what I wanted at the mall when I was a kid. But the slow kind of tears that sort of bubbled up and stung my eyes before they ran hot down my cheeks. My mom looked at me blubbering like some kind of wimp, and shook her head. "Don't even try," she warned. "Tears are *not* going to make me feel bad for you. This is your fault."

Then she turned and walked out, muttering something under her breath.

At that moment, the only thing I could think about was how much I hated my mom. And how much I hated my dad, for getting this stupid job and never hanging out with me anymore. And I also hated myself, for turning into a huge baby and losing control in front of my mom.

But after a few minutes of letting myself wallow in self-pity, I realized it was time to do what I do best: take charge and make things go my way. How hard could it be to make these people adore me?

Chapter Six

I rubbed at my cheeks, trying to erase the tear streaks from my skin. They were a visible reminder that my mom was the one person who could always make me feel totally worthless. As I pulled a brush through my hair, someone knocked at the cabin door.

"Hello?" I heard Bailey yell through the screen door. "Isabella?"

I snuffled one last time, making sure I was done crying. Tears weren't going to help my cause with these people. Then I headed out into the living room, where Mom was already talking with Bailey.

"I'm sure she'd love to go canoeing," I heard her say. "Izzy was just saying how much she wanted to do something with all of you."

I stared at my mom, speechless. I was so *not* just saying that. My mom was making me look desperate. That I didn't need.

"Oh, great!" Bailey chirped. "We need one more person for Canoe Wars, or the weights will be all weird in the boats. Which is totally not fair."

"Sounds fun," I grumbled, without any enthusiasm at all. I wasn't going to act all chipper and let my mom win. "Let's go." I pushed through the busted front door and wrapped my arm through Bailey's. Then I dragged my new friend—really, that's what Bailey was going to have to be now that I didn't have a phone—down the steps, along the path, and toward the lake.

Bailey followed behind me. Like a puppy. Pitiful.

"So what is Canoe Wars, anyway?" I asked, as we neared the lake.

Bailey grinned at me, totally oblivious to the fact that I was not at all happy. But even though her clueless grin bugged me, there was something mischievous in her smile that I found the tiniest bit intriguing. Bailey shook her head and said, "You'll see."

"Tell me what it is, or I'm not doing it," I said.

Bailey raised her eyebrows. After a long pause, where

neither of us said anything, Bailey laughed. Finally, she said, "You don't have to do this, you know. I'm not going to force you to get in the boat."

"No," I said, softening. "I'll do it. I just want to know what I'm getting into before I agree to do something stupid."

"I already told you, you'll find out." Bailey reached down and scratched at a bug bite on her leg.

Fine. I would play by her rules. This once.

"And just so you know," Bailey said, wrinkling her nose so her freckles all bunched up into a little cluster of spots in the center of her face. "It probably wouldn't kill you to be a little nicer to everyone. We all know you don't want to be here—but maybe you could try to have a decent time, just for the month? We're all stuck at the lake together, and it's going to be a lot more fun for everyone if you ditch the attitude." She smiled, all smug. "When we get back to school, you can act however you want to act and be who you want to be. But for now, just try to be a little less awful. Okay?"

My mouth dropped open. *That* I was not expecting. No one—except my parents—had *ever* spoken to me like that before. I didn't even know how to respond.

Suddenly, Ava bounded up beside us. "Oh, good," she said. "You're in?" She looked at me expectantly.

After a long moment, I nodded. I wasn't sure what I was agreeing to—Bailey's request, or Ava's question—but my answer to both was yes. Bailey was right. It was just a month, and there was no reason I couldn't pretend to be friends with these girls for the month. It's not like anyone at school had to know about anything that happened over the summer. Everything *would* go back to normal when school started. I'd make sure of it.

Ava and Bailey skipped the rest of the way down the hill and jogged onto the beach. Brennan, Madeline, and Zach were standing onshore beside two enormous aluminum canoes.

"What are the teams?" Bailey blurted out, strapping a life jacket on.

Brennan looked at me suspiciously. "The most important question is, who gets the new girl?"

"I assume you're talking about me? My name is Izzy." I tried to act like it didn't matter that I was going to be the last person picked for their little teams. "How long have you all known each other, anyway?"

"Six years?" Ava said quietly, answering my question with a question instead of a confident statement. It was no wonder she was always getting teased and tortured at school. It was almost like she wanted people to think she was a total door-mat. "At least, that's when I first met everyone . . . I guess? But Bailey's mom has been doing this summer retreat thing with the firm since before Bailey was even born."

"My mom's maternity leave—the summer she had me—was at the lake, actually," Bailey said quickly. "So I've been coming here my whole life. Brennan and Zach's mom just started working at the agency a year or two ago, so this is their second summer. Levi, who you met at the bonfire, comes every other year—he spent last summer at his mom's house in Chicago, but this year his dad and stepmom got August, so he's here again, which is super-fun. But he's in town with his stepmom this afternoon, which is why we're short one person for Canoe Wars."

"Oh," I said, trying to digest Bailey's information dump. The girl really liked to talk. "O-*kay*."

"So let's do this!" Brennan said. "I call Zach and Madeline!"

"That's so not fair," Ava whined. "They're the strongest. And, uh . . ." She glanced at me.

Bailey piped up, "But we're the smartest. You're going down, Bren." She narrowed her eyes at him, and put her hands on her hips. She began to growl, which made every-one start laughing, and once again, I found myself sort of intrigued by Bailey. I seriously hoped she wasn't trying to flirt with Brennan, though. Because if she was, she was going about it all wrong.

And also, if anyone was going to flirt with Brennan, it ought to be me.

"Get in," Bailey instructed. "Sit in the middle." She pointed, and I climbed into the center of one of the canoes while it was still pulled up onshore. Bailey and Ava pushed it out into the swimming area. When they were standing about waist-deep in the water, they got on either side of the canoe, lifted one leg into the boat, and climbed in.

"How did you do that without the canoe tipping?" I asked. It was pretty impressive. "I thought canoes were supposed to be super tippy?"

"They are tippy," Bailey said. "That's the whole point of Canoe Wars. But Ava and I have had a lot of practice doing this—as long as we climb in at the same time from opposite sides, our bodies cancel each other out and the canoe doesn't tip. Teamwork."

"Where are the oars?" I asked, looking back toward shore.

"Oars?" Ava snorted. "You mean paddles?"

"Does it matter?" I snapped.

"Kind of," Ava said. She was still snickering. Apparently

I needed to read up on whittling and canoe paddles. "Oars are for a rowboat. Paddles are for a canoe. But we don't use either for this game. It's all about sneakery." While she'd been talking, the canoe had floated out to the far edge of the swimming area, near the buoys. I shifted, trying to get comfortable on the bottom of the boat. But every time I moved, the canoe swayed, so I felt like I couldn't even wiggle my foot.

Suddenly, I felt something thump the bottom of the canoe. I screamed and jumped up, moving as fast as I would if piranhas were attacking. *Were* piranhas attacking? Did lakes *have* piranhas? I knew that lakes sometimes had creepy-looking brown fish with whiskers, and that was bad enough. I saw some at the zoo once, and honestly, they were spookier than sharks. I leapt up, eager to escape whatever it was that had knocked against me through the canoe. As I stood up, the boat rocked wildly to the side, thrown off balance by my sudden movement. I flung my hands out to the side, trying to regain my balance, but it was no use. My arms circled in the air, and I felt my body tipping until—

Splash!

The canoe and I both went over. As soon as I resurfaced, I gasped and screamed. "What *was* that?" My feet kicked at the surface of the water, and I flapped my arms to stay afloat. I was drowning, I was just sure of it.

That's when I realized Bailey and Ava were both standing in water chest-deep beside me, smirking as they watched me freak out. "Brennan," Bailey explained. "*That* was Brennan. And we just lost the first round of Canoe Wars."

I was so confused. "No, I mean, something thumped the bottom of the canoe. Like, a catfish or a huge turtle or something. I felt it!" I kicked my legs wildly under the water, trying to make sure nothing would sneak up and bite me in the thigh. Suddenly, something did. "Aah! There it is again."

I panicked, fear making me weak and wobbly and near tears (for the second time that day). But moments later, Brennan popped out of the murky water less than a foot away from us. He held up one of Levi's whittled sticks in his hand, and poked it in our direction.

"That was *you*?" I spluttered, as embarrassment washed over me. It was then that I finally understood that Brennan was the thing that knocked on the bottom of the canoe. Not a turtle. Not a piranha. Lobster Boy.

"I don't think anyone's ever lost Canoe Wars that fast," Brennan said, shaking his head. "Like, ever in the history of Canoe Wars. That was the saddest thing I've ever seen."

I folded my arms tightly across my chest.

"Give us another chance," Ava said, as she and Bailey worked to right our canoe again. I stood shivering in waist-deep water. After a few tugs, Bailey and Ava were able to turn the canoe upright again. But now it was almost completely full of water. Somehow, the thing continued to float even though it was still partially underwater. "You're up one. Let's do best of three."

"This is a stupid game," I announced, because it was the truth. "Brennan tipped our canoe. How is that fair?"

Brennan held his hands in the air, like he was a criminal under arrest. "I did not tip your canoe," he said firmly. "*You* tipped your canoe."

"But . . . ," I argued. "But you were under our canoe, right? You were thunking us, and trying to freak me out, and you totally tipped our boat."

Bailey laughed, and I shot her a look. It obviously didn't do the trick, since Bailey kept laughing. She covered her mouth, but we could all still hear her gasping laugh. Finally, she said, "Brennan would have to be seriously strong to lift our boat up in the air and tip us. Honestly, we went over because you got spooked and stood up. Don't you know you're *never* supposed to stand up in a canoe?" She scolded me like I was a child.

"See, the point of Canoe Wars is to try to get the other team to dump without actually touching their boat with any kind of force."

"Those are really vague rules," I said, shivering even more. The sky had been filled with big cotton-ball clouds all day, but now they were getting darker, and one was parked right in front of the sun. Suddenly, it felt sort of chilly in the water. "So you're just supposed to try to scare the other team enough that they just—*whoop!*—fall out of their boat on their own? Isn't that sort of simple?"

"Well," Ava said politely, "it's not really supposed to be that simple. . . . No one's ever actually just knocked on the bottom of someone else's canoe and gotten them to fall into the lake. Normally, it takes a little more than that. Usually, we have to push people with paddles and make big waves and stuff. But even *that* usually isn't enough to make a team tip." Ava shrugged. She reminded me of a teacher, the way she was acting all preachy. "Most of the time, Canoe Wars doesn't end until someone adds an extra challenge that makes it harder to stay in your own boat. Like, we all have to stand up and dance in our canoes or something."

"This is a seriously stupid game," I said, rolling my eyes.

I could feel myself pouting, so I pulled my lower lip between my teeth and chewed.

"Then don't play," Brennan said with a shrug. "Obviously, Ava and Bailey are a lot better off with an unbalanced team than they are with you in their boat."

Brennan stared at me, and I crossed my arms and stared back. I couldn't believe I'd ever thought he was cute. What a jerk! He didn't have to be so rude about everything. Eventually, I blinked and looked around at the others. Ava and Bailey were both back in our canoe—even though it was still half-underwater. They both looked at me, their faces filled with pity. Pity I didn't need. Madeline and Zach were just sitting patiently in the other canoe, watching to see what might happen. Bailey tipped her head, as if to say, *In or out?*

"Fine," I said sullenly. I was cold and embarrassed, but I wasn't a quitter. "Best two out of three."

"We're so glad you'll stoop to join us, Your Highness," Brennan said with an arrogant smile. He gestured to the sunken canoe and bowed. "May I help you into your chariot?"

Chapter Seven

~~~~~~~~~~~~~~~~~~~~~~~~~~~~~

What an arrogant jerk!

I really wanted to show Brennan that I wasn't a total princess, and that I could play their stupid canoe game. But even though I sat as still as possible and tried really, really hard to *not* rock the boat, our team still lost the next round of Canoe Wars in less than two minutes. Apparently, Bailey and Ava made a critical error when they left me alone to protect the half-submerged canoe while they swam underwater to try to make a move on Brennan, Madeline, and Zach.

"Just sit as still as you can," Bailey instructed as they swam away. Choppy waves lapped at the side of the canoe, making it rock back and forth. But I sat still, my hands wrapped tightly around the sides of the boat. I worked on conjuring up my Zen focus. I had to prove myself.

"We'll be back in two seconds," Ava promised, looking back. "Just don't move while we're gone."

But as soon as she and Bailey were positioned on either side of Brennan's canoe, Zach popped up out of the water, right by my seat. "Boo!" He screamed into my ear and threw a live crayfish into the boat. The creepy thing zipped around in the water, its little pincers opening and closing. I screamed too, and flailed around in the watery canoe, trying to keep as far as possible from the creepy crayfish. I swished my body back and forth in the water inside the canoe, but the crayfish acted like it was hunting me for dinner. Finally, unable to escape the snapping little beast, I jumped up and hopped around, trying to keep my toes out of its claws. But once the boat started rocking, I couldn't figure out how to keep it from going over. Within seconds, I'd rolled out into neck-deep water, and the canoe floated upside down in the lake once again.

I watched the crayfish roll out of the canoe beside me, then swim lazily to the bottom of the lake. I was totally skeeved out, since marine life was freaky. But more than anything, I felt picked on.

"Best three of five?" Ava suggested hopefully. When no one said anything, she muttered, "Maybe later."

I'm not dim. I knew that "maybe later" meant "maybe later when Izzy's not around." I felt the sting of rejection, though no one had actually said they didn't want me there outright. It was almost worse that no one just came out and told me to leave. I felt like one of the cling-on girls that always tried to hang out with Heidi and Sylvie and me—there were a few of them in our grade that just didn't get that they weren't welcome, no matter how many times we'd made it clear.

I knew I was like one of those girls now. No one needed or wanted me there, but no one had the guts to just come out and say it.

Even though I wanted to go back to my cabin and hide, I decided to help Ava and Bailey dump the water out of our canoe and drag it back to shore. But every time I tried to help, I just kept tipping the thing again. So finally, Bailey told me to wait onshore while they did it themselves. "It's easier with just two," she lied, smiling at me like I was some sort of idiot.

I tried to think of an excuse to get out of there, but found it impossible to come up with anything that wouldn't make me look like I was a sore loser. I considered saying I had to go back to my cabin to put on sunscreen, but the giant clouds had completely obstructed the sun, and I knew it would sound like a hollow excuse. So I unhooked my life jacket and hung it over the fence that ran along the tree line. I leaned against a fence post and watched the clouds rolling in over the lake, wondering if this is how it felt when Heidi and Sylvie and I wouldn't let people sit at our lunch table. I felt like an outsider, like I couldn't do or say anything right, and it made me nauseous.

Just as Bailey and Ava pulled the empty canoe up onto shore, a low rumble of thunder growled in the sky. The clouds, which had seemed relatively puffy and unthreatening while we were playing the game, suddenly turned dark and ominous. Green and orange swirled together in the sky, and lightning lit up the horizon across the lake. The adults who were working and chatting on the dock nearby quickly gathered up their papers. I saw my dad glance over at me as he hustled away to safety with the other adults. *Thanks for the concern about me being in the lake during a storm, Dad*, I thought bitterly. I remembered one time when I was little, my dad and I had been caught out in the backyard as a storm rolled in. He and I had stared up at the sky together until the first drops of rain hit our cheeks, then he'd wrapped me up inside his sweatshirt and we'd watched movies on the couch all afternoon. He knew how much I hated storms, so he'd turned the sound up extra loud so I couldn't hear the thunder.

"We should probably get inside," I said. I especially hate the kind of storms that creep up and surprise me. The ones that came out of nowhere seemed meaner and uglier, somehow.

Suddenly, another crack of thunder, closer this time, shook the sky above us. Then the clouds opened, and rain poured down. Even though we were already wet, everyone shrieked. I chased Bailey and Ava up the hill toward the cluster of cabins. Brennan and Zach took off one way at the end of the path, while we all went the other way. Madeline split off from us to run to the cabin she shared with Ava and their dad, but Bailey grabbed me and Ava and yelled, "Come with me! Thunderstorms scare me, and Mom's working all afternoon. Please?"

I didn't have time to react. I just let Bailey tug me down an unfamiliar wooded path as another thunderclap popped above us. The wind whipped through the forested area that surrounded our cabins, and as lightning blazed in the sky above us, I wondered about the safety of our ramshackle cabins. Could a huge storm blow them over, or rip them out of the ground, à la *Wizard of Oz*?

I suddenly realized I had to get Coco. My puppy had never been in a thunderstorm before, and I didn't want her stuck in the cabin, scared and alone. My mom had made it very clear that Coco was *my* dog, and any dog care and maintenance was *my* responsibility. "Can I bring my dog to your cabin?" I had to yell so Bailey could hear me through the pounding rain.

"Of course!" Bailey yelled back. Her eyes were wide and scared, and I could tell she was more freaked out by thunderstorms than I was. But even though it was obvious she wanted to get inside, Bailey said, "We'll come with you to get her!"

Ava and Bailey followed as I ran to my cabin. For a moment, I thought about suggesting that we could all go to my cabin, since we were almost there and the rain was really slamming into us. But I knew my mom would freak out if we all tromped in, wet and dripping. Besides, I was still mad at my mom, and I was pretty relieved I had an excuse to stay away.

I ran up the steps to the Cardinal cabin and popped open the screen door. Coco was shivering, curled into a tight ball right by the doormat, so I just leaned down and scooped her up into my arms. I wrapped her in a dry towel, then ran back down the stairs and into the rain again. Coco shook inside the towel, so I held her tighter, pulling her against my chest to shield her from the rain. I chased after Bailey as she and Ava ran past several cabins and then down a small hill. The next crack of thunder made the ground shake, and I was almost sure the earth was going to open up in front of me.

Coco wriggled in my arms. She poked her wet little nose out of the towel just as the next blast of lightning lit up the sky. Panicked, she jumped out of my arms, shaking the towel off her body. In the moment before she ran, I saw that her usually floppy ears were pressed tight against her head. "Coco!" I screamed. The rain was coming down in sheets, hitting me at an angle. I could hardly see the cabins on either side of me. The lake was just a swirling mass of waves and rain at the bottom of the hill. And Coco was a dark blur, zigging and zagging between trees. In less than an instant, I couldn't see her anymore at all. "Coco! Come back!"

Bailey and Ava both stopped running and turned back to see what I was screaming about. "My dog is gone!" I told them. Fear crippled my reflexes, turning me slow and useless. I bent down to pick up the towel on the ground, the one that my puppy had been wrapped safely in just moments before. It was warm and soaking wet. "I have to find her."

Without a moment of hesitation, both Bailey and Ava ran off in different directions, jumping into action. Seeing them react helped shake me out of my stupor. We all shouted for Coco, our voices muffled by the rain. I could feel the raindrops hitting my back, stinging the bare skin my swimsuit didn't cover, and bouncing off my head.

Thunder rocked the sky again. In the silence that followed, I thought I could hear Coco whining from somewhere nearby, but I couldn't see anything except rain and trees. The way everything hung heavy and wet around me made me feel claustrophobic, and my breath became shallow. It felt like the world was closing in on me as I realized I'd lost my dog in a forest full of terrible creatures and beasts. I turned in circles, searching the dark woods around me for any sign of her. In the weeks Coco had been mine, she had hardly left my side. She wasn't the sort of dog who wandered off—she was a cuddler, a snuggly puppy who would rather squeeze into the only open space in my twin bed than stretch out in her own fluffy, spacious dog bed on the floor.

A tangle of lightning lit up the sky again, but I still couldn't see where my dog might have run off. I thought again about the raccoons I knew came out at night—the ones that ate the barbecue remains—and about the other things that might be hiding in the woods that surrounded us. I choked on my own voice as I yelled again, and my cry was carried away by the wind.

Bailey rounded the corner of a cabin, and as lightning flashed, I could see that she looked terror-stricken. "You can go inside," I yelled. Bailey had told us she was scared of storms, and here she was, stuck out in the whipping wind and pounding rain. I understood how horrible she must feel, being stuck out here. "I'll keep looking for her."

"No way," Bailey said, her chin thrust forward. She ran off again, yelling, "Coco!"

Suddenly, Ava cried out to us from near one of the cabins. "I found her! She's at Bailey's cabin!"

I ran, with Bailey close behind. When I got near, I saw that Coco had found shelter under the crumbling bottom step leading up to Bailey's cabin. I reached down and held out my arms. "We're going inside," I cooed, trying to coax my puppy out of her hiding spot. "Come here, girl." Whimpering, Coco reluctantly squirmed out from under the step, and I swept her up in my arms.

Bailey, Ava, and I ran up the steps to Bailey's cabin, and pushed open the screen door. Water dripped off our bodies and pooled on the floor, but Bailey didn't seem to care. She flopped down in one of the wooden chairs and closed her eyes.

"Thank you," I said, hugging Coco tight against my chest. Relief flooded my body, and I buried my face in Coco's neck.

"No problem," Ava said quietly. She pulled a couple of dry towels off the kitchen counter. She offered one to me, then handed one to Bailey. "I'm glad we found her."

Once we'd all dried off, Bailey pulled the blankets off her bed and threw them in a cushy pile on the hard wooden couch in the living room. As the storm raged outside, we all tucked in together under heaps of fleece blankets with Coco stretched out, fast asleep across our laps.

Chapter Eight

~~~~~~~~~~~~~~~

After five minutes inside Bailey's cabin, I was uncomfortable. I was squished in between Ava, whose personality seemed to have washed away completely in the rain, and Bailey, who wouldn't stop talking. Bailey was going on and on about her brother, who was five years older than us and apparently starting college in a few weeks. I literally couldn't have cared less about Bailey's brother, who sounded boring, and I wished Bailey would remember to stop to take a breath between stories.

I let my mind wander, wondering what Heidi and Sylvie were doing, and wishing I was there doing it with them. I didn't want to be stuck inside a steamy cabin, trapped by the rain. At times, while Bailey was talking, I felt like I was volunteering for some sort of charity. It almost seemed like I should get a whole load of good karma points for spending time with these girls and listening to their inconsequential stories.

But every time I convinced myself that I was doing Ava and Bailey some sort of favor by hanging out with them, I thought about the look on Bailey's face as she'd searched for Coco in the rain. And I thought of the way Ava had tried to make me feel less like a useless lump when I was trying to help them get the canoe out of the lake. If Heidi had been there, she would have freaked about her hair in the rain and run to her cabin without even looking back. And Sylvie would have relentlessly teased me for even getting *in* a canoe. If she'd been there when I fell out of it—twice—Sylvie would have howled with laughter and made sure everyone else did too.

From what I could tell, Bailey and Ava were *nice*. Too nice. But, I wondered, were they nice because they were naive and simple, or nice because they wanted something? I had another few weeks to figure it out, and I was sort of looking forward to the opportunity to study these two strange girls. No one was just nice. The world didn't work that way.

"What about you, Izzy?" Bailey said, opening her big eyes wide. "Do you have any brothers or sisters?"

Oh, man, was she still talking about her brother? Oy.

"No, it's just me," I said aloud. "My parents always say I'm more work than they ever signed up for, so it's a good thing I'm an only child."

Bailey pulled her eyebrows together. "They say that?"

"Sometimes," I said with a shrug. "But it's sort of true."

"Still," Ava added quietly, "your parents are supposed to love you unconditionally."

I cracked up. "Are you *serious*?" I continued to laugh, as Bailey and Ava both looked at me with vacant expressions. "No, seriously . . . you really think that? That your parents are supposed to love you unconditionally? Do you live in some sort of TV movie or something?"

"No," Bailey said, blushing.

"Does your family have dinner together every night?" I asked, still laughing.

"Yeah," Ava said simply. "Don't you?"

I actually snorted at the thought of my family sitting down to eat together every night. We would have nothing to say to each other. Every once in a while, my dad would make it home before seven, and we'd all sit at the table together, all three of us quickly shoveling in our food while my dad talked about work. But that happened so rarely that I couldn't even remember the last time we'd done it. That's why it had seemed so ridiculous that my dad had insisted Mom and I come on this trip with him at all.

It's not like we're a family that *does* things together. When I was little, my dad and I used to take bike rides together on the weekends or go swimming—just the two of us—after dinner in the summer. But now neither of us has time for that. The only regular communication I've had with either of my parents involves them nagging and me being forced to listen mutely or fight back.

"I bet you both have the kind of families that get each other stuff like hand-knit sweaters and candles for Christmas, don't you?" I blurted out, feeling defensive. The whole idea repulsed me, the thought that someone's family would gather around the Christmas tree, opening gifts made with love—everyone oohing and aahing over stupid homemade trinkets. But even though I wanted to believe it was a stupid concept, a huge waste of time and wool, I had sort of always wished for a family like that. Like the families on TV, or in books. "Do you get excited when Santa leaves a fresh toothbrush for you under the tree?" I couldn't resist picking a little more, making fun of them for something I didn't have, just because it seemed so crazy.

I felt myself growing bitter, as I conjured up images of Madeline and Ava in matching sweaters, singing songs around the campfire, holding hands with their mommy. And then I pictured Bailey and Big Boss Erica, hugging and going out to dinner to celebrate Bailey's super-duper report card. I despised them for what they had, but I also envied them. Not that I wanted to hold hands with my crab of a mother, but I did sometimes wish that we could talk without ragging on each other all the time. And I wished my dad would look at me the way he used to, before he got too busy to even like me anymore. When we used to do things together just for fun and not just for show.

Neither Bailey nor Ava said anything, but I could sense that I'd crossed a line. I was picking just for the sake of picking . . . and I suddenly felt like my mom. I'd sensed weakness and pounced, even though no one was pushing back. "I'm sorry," I said, realizing as I said it that it was true. "I don't know why I'm making fun of your families. I guess I'm just annoyed by mine."

"That's not my family," Bailey blurted out. "I don't know what kind of world you think I live in, but it's certainly not a hand-knit-sweater and craft family. My mom's the president of an incredibly busy advertising agency. I actually have to get her *assistant* to put my swim meets on her BlackBerry calendar. You think she has time to knit?"

I shrugged. "I guess not."

"And my parents are divorced. I live with just my dad," Ava muttered. "Madeline and I are lucky if Dad remembers to buy new toothbrushes at all—ever. He's so spacey that last year he bought Madeline a shirt that was size 5T. Like he forgot that she was nine already and had outgrown the toddler section five years ago. She practically needs a bra, and Dad's buying her baby clothes." Ava grinned, then we all started laughing.

In that moment, as we all laughed together about our parents' craziness, I realized Bailey and Ava were real people. Not just wannabes, flitting around somewhere outside my circle, looking for a way in. The image of these nice (albeit boring) girls in polished, plain, pitiful lives was momentarily washed away—and they became Ava and Bailey, who were maybe, kind of . . . not awful. For the first time, I realized, I was actually interested in getting to know them. It was possible that they might actually be decent enough to make the end of the summer not totally stink.

"You know what we should do?" Bailey said, hopping off the couch in a sudden burst of energy. Coco looked up, her eyes only half-open as she shifted into Bailey's open spot on the couch. "Let's dance."

"Yes!" Ava squealed. I had never heard her get that loud.

I thought Ava only spoke in whispers, apologetic little bits of conversation that no one was supposed to hear. "Can we work on my routine?"

"What routine?" I asked, my eyes wide. I suddenly worried that maybe You, Only Better had some sort of talent show at the end of the month. No one would get me to participate in something like that for all the money in the world. And the idea of my dad up onstage, singing Black Eyed Peas or Adele or something, made me want to vomit. My dad was totally the kind of guy who would sing in front of everyone too. He was the show-offy "Cool Guy," the brand of dad who always wants to make everyone think he's really fun and easygoing. He isn't. Every time he acted like that lately, it was one hundred percent for show. "What are you talking about?" I repeated. "A gymnastics routine or something?"

Ava looked at Bailey, and Bailey shrugged. "Just tell her. She'll find out eventually."

"Tell me what?" I asked.

"I'm trying out for Southwest's dance team this fall," Ava said. "Promise you won't make fun of me. . . ."

"Why would I make fun of you?"

"Because you're Isabella Caravelli." Bailey stared me down. "That's what you do."

I shrugged. That was true. And in fact, I really did want to laugh about the idea of someone like Ava actually trying out for our school's dance team. Ava would never make the team, not in a million years. She would be eaten alive at auditions. But instead of saying that—which would have been the honest thing to say—I said, "Can I see you dance? I'll help you if I can."

Ava squealed, and ran into Bailey's room to turn on the music.

"Are you trying out for dance this year?" Bailey asked me. She was shuffling around in the kitchen, looking for snacks while Ava got ready.

I shook my head. "No, I have soccer." This was a lie that easily rolled off my tongue by now. I've somehow convinced everyone that I'm totally committed to soccer, or I definitely would be on the dance team. But the truth is, I have never and will never try out, because I know I'd never make the team. I'm a terrible dancer—like, dead-fish-flopping-around-in-the-bottom-of-a-boat bad. I've never even figured out how to make my body do simple tumbling stuff, like cartwheels, so there's no way I'm going to humiliate myself by trying to learn a complicated dance routine and then mess up in front of everyone.

The tough thing is, I'm practically the only one of my friends who *isn't* trying out. I don't like to think about how horrible it will be if they all make the team, then start hanging out without me. But only a few people make the dance team each year, so I know it isn't very likely. Everyone knows Heidi has no rhythm and Sylvie always cracks under pressure, so I'm not too worried about them making it. I'm kind of counting on both of them to mess up, actually.

I know you're supposed to support your friends, but it's hard to do when I know they'll both be better off if they just don't make it. Then nothing has to change with us, and my best friends will still need me just as much as they always have.

"Soccer?" Bailey said, looking at me curiously. "Can't you do both?"

Yes, I could. But I choose not to. "Nope," I said, with no further explanation. I hoped Bailey would just butt out.

All of a sudden, a pulsing dance mix pumped through the wooden cabin. I tapped my feet, waiting on the couch as Ava prepared to enter.

"Action!" Bailey cried, clapping from the kitchen. She pulled her video camera out and pointed it toward the door of her bedroom.

Ava burst out from behind the bedroom curtain, her usually mousy expression gone. In its place was a huge smile. She leapt from the kitchen into the living room, her arms outstretched. She jumped and whirled, tossed her hair and kicked her feet. When the song ended, she landed in a full splits, with her arms straight above her head. Then her whole body collapsed forward onto the floor, her face flushed. After a few seconds, she peeked up from under her hair. "So?"

"So that was amazing!" I said honestly. I've seen Heidi's and Sylvie's routines, and they aren't even in the same league as Ava's. "I did *not* expect you to dance like that."

"I guess that's a compliment?" Ava whispered.

"I guess so," I agreed. Sometimes I even surprised myself.

Chapter Nine

~~~~~~~~~~~~

W hat's the deal with Brennan?" I asked the next day as I stretched out on the dock beside Ava and Bailey. Now that I'd come to terms with the fact that we were just a summer thing, I was able to relax a little more when I was with them. They were pretty fun, and they definitely beat hanging out with my mom.

"He's super-cute, isn't he?" Bailey giggled.

"I guess," I said, keeping my eyes hidden behind my sunglasses. I didn't want to admit just *how* cute I thought he was, since Brennan wasn't really very nice to me the day before during Canoe Wars. I had a feeling I wasn't exactly his favorite girl at the resort. "Is he our age?"

"No, he's going into eighth grade," Ava said. "He goes to Hill."

Hill was the other middle school in our district. Sometimes we played them in soccer—but I didn't know anyone who went there.

"I *wish* he went to Southwest," Bailey said, pulling her hair back into a messy ponytail. "Maybe then he'd realize I'm not just some kid he spends summers·with at the lake."

"Oh!" I said, as realization hit. "You like him!"

"No!" Bailey said immediately. But the flush in her cheeks gave her away. "I mean, sure, he's cute, but it's not like I'd ever have a chance with him. Someone like you might, maybe, but not me."

I studied Bailey through my sunglasses, realizing she was making excuses for why she couldn't or shouldn't have a crush on Brennan. It bothered me, the way she was dismissing herself, like she wasn't good enough for him. "Why do you say that?" I demanded. "Why would you think you wouldn't ever have a chance with him?"

Bailey shrugged. "I just—I just don't."

There was something in the way she said it that made me think that maybe she sort of *did* think she had a chance. But something was obviously holding her back. "You really believe that?" I lifted my sunglasses so I could look right at her. "Because I think you don't."

Bailey laughed. "I mean, yeah, maybe he sometimes flirts with me a little bit. But that doesn't mean anything. He flirts with everyone. It's no big deal."

"Well," I said, casually dropping my sunglasses back over my eyes. "I definitely think he's cute. And I think we should figure out who—if anyone—he *does* like here. There's no sense in letting a good guy go to waste all month, right?" I realized that if Bailey wasn't going to go after him, well, then I might as well flirt with him myself. It was good practice for real guys, if nothing else.

"How are you going to do that?" Ava asked, her mouth an O of surprise. I'd started to realize that Ava almost always looked surprised and scared. "Are you just going to ask him?"

"Of course I'm not just going to ask him!" I said, rolling my eyes. Suddenly, I had an idea. "Let's *all* flirt with him for the next week and see how things turn out." I liked this plan. I loved the idea of all of us flirting with Brennan, trying to get him to pick one of us over the others. The main reason I loved the idea is, I always won games like this. And I had no doubt I'd win at this, too. I knew there was no way Bailey or Ava was better at getting a guy's attention than I am. Hopefully, they would appreciate the chance to learn something about flirting from me. They should be psyched that I was willing to teach them a thing or two!

"I think that sounds awful," Bailey said, shaking her head.

"What . . . are you afraid of a little flirting?" I teased. "Do you not know *how* to flirt?" That was probably it. If she really was afraid to flirt, I felt bad for her. I was doing her a favor by showing her how this worked!

Bailey didn't laugh at my teasing, like Heidi or Sylvie would have. She almost looked like I'd offended her. "Yes, I know how to flirt," she said coolly. "It just seems like one of us is going to end up feeling awful at the end of the week if we do that."

I considered her point. My friends and I did this sort of thing all the time. Sure, someone got hurt at the end of one of our little competitions, but whoever it was eventually got over it. There are winners and losers in life; that's just the way it is, and people have to figure that out. Besides, I usually won— and that made our games a lot more fun for me. "Yeah, someone's feelings might get a little hurt," I agreed, lying back on my towel. I didn't like the look on Bailey's face. It was making me uncomfortable, like I'd disappointed her. "I just thought it would be fun. You can play or you can not play. But I'm going to try to get Brennan to notice me."

. I caught Ava and Bailey glancing at each other. I glared at them from behind my dark glasses. "What?" I demanded. Clearly, they were upset about something. They were both so transparent, it was easy for me to read them. But I figured neither of them would have the guts to actually say anything to me, so it didn't really matter *what* they were thinking.

Ava pushed herself up and sat cross-legged beside Bailey. She squeaked out, "You don't think you're being rude?"

"Why is that rude?" I asked. I had no idea what Ava was so upset about. Neither she nor Bailey was actively going after Brennan, so why was he suddenly off-limits to me, too?

"Bailey *just* told you she thinks he's cute. And now, suddenly, you're going to try to get him to like you?" Ava's voice went up an octave. "Maybe that's how you do things with your friends, but that's not how we treat each other. It's just rude." She sat up straighter and said, "No offense, but if you're going to keep acting the way you do at school, I don't really want to hang out with you." She squared her shoulders and tried to look tough, but I could see that she was shaking.

"Fine," I said, keeping my voice even.

But it really wasn't fine. I had just started to like Ava and Bailey, and having them tell me they didn't want to spend time with me was hurtful. I'd discovered that they were easy and relaxing to be around, and I could feel myself unwind a little bit when I spent time with them. I could just *be*, and I didn't have to work so hard to control everything around me. Something about them made me wish I was a better person. And I guess it was true that a nicer person probably wouldn't design a game to try to steal someone else's crush. "Actually," I said, speaking quietly, embarrassed, "it's not fine. You're right."

"Ava's usually right about stuff like that," Bailey added. "She's a really good friend."

And Izzy's not. I finished Bailey's comment for her in my head. Sometimes I knew I wasn't the greatest friend. But it was hard. There was a fine line between being a doormat and being a good friend, and I just don't want to put myself in a position where people might push me around. So I always push first—that way I always have the upper hand. It's all about maintaining control. But I was starting to realize control didn't matter quite as much at the lake, and maybe I could just sit back and hang out for a few weeks.

"So let's forget the flirting challenge," I said. "Pretend I never suggested it, okay?"

Bailey shrugged. "I guess."

"Seriously," I said. "Please, just forget I said it." I realized it sounded like I was begging, but maybe that was okay. It was possible I had to do some things I didn't usually like to do if I wanted to make the summer with these girls work. Maybe it would take a little begging and a lot of holding my tongue if I wanted to avoid spending every minute inside the cabin with my mom. "Maybe Ava and I can help you with Brennan somehow?"

Bailey didn't look convinced. "Really?"

"Sure," I offered. "It might be kind of fun. It will be like a project."

"I'm not your project," Bailey said, her mouth set. "If you think you're doing me some sort of favor, don't. I don't need your charity, and I certainly don't need lessons from you on how to get people to like me."

Wow.

Neither of these girls was at *all* like I thought they were going to be. Bailey was actually a little like a pitbull sometimes. She was pretty fierce and definitely stood up for what she believed in. Kind of like me. But not.

"Maybe we should start over," I suggested, trying to figure out how I was supposed to go about offering up a truce, when really, I was probably the reason everything had gone wrong in the first place. "I think we got off to a bad start. *I* got off to a bad start." I sat up on my towel, pulled off my sunglasses, and looked both Bailey and Ava in the eye. "I'm Izzy," I said with a smile. "It's really nice to meet you. I hope we can be friends." I was surprised something so cheesy was coming out of my mouth.

But as I said it, the thing that surprised me the most was just how much I meant it.

Chapter Ten

~~~~~~~~~~~~~~~~~~~~~~

I guess all it took was admitting that I'd been sort of—okay, maybe a touch more than *sort of*—rude at the beginning of the month. Because after that day on the dock, Bailey and Ava and I got along really well. We spent most of our days on the beach or in the water. A lot of days we hung out with Brennan and Zach, or Levi, and often Madeline, but many times it was just the three of us. I was still completely useless at Canoe Wars, even after six more rounds of practice. My team *always* lost—but I had fun anyway, and everyone liked cracking jokes at my expense.

Most afternoons, Bailey, Ava, and I spent an hour or two at Ava's cabin, helping her practice her dance routine. Bailey always had her video camera with her, to take rehearsal shots of Ava while she danced. Sometimes we'd huddle around the little video screen afterward and give Ava silly tips on what she could improve upon. Neither Bailey nor I were of any use in the "real dance advice" department—so we always tried to one-up each other with really ridiculous suggestions, like suggesting she attempt to do the whole dance with frozen joints or that she complete her routine without smiling.

When I finally broke down and confessed that I had two left feet, Ava was really excited about showing me how to dance. Neither she nor Bailey teased me at all, they just let me stand behind them and mirror their steps while they moved around the cramped spaces in their cabins. Both Bailey and I learned Ava's routine inside and out, though neither of us looked nearly as good as Ava did when she was totally in the zone. She was amazing. I was . . . shaky, at best.

But the best part was, I didn't even care if I looked stupid. Something about Bailey and Ava made me not really care that much about how silly I looked or sounded. They didn't judge me, which made it so simple to just hang out and have a good time.

And that was the other amazing thing . . . I *was* having a good time.

Every night, we spent our evenings around the campfire

hanging out with everyone else, including Brennan . . . who seemed to be totally into Bailey! Operation: Flirt was totally under way, and I was really impressed by Bailey's guy skills. Brennan seemed to like her sort of awkward, tomboyish flirtiness, and Ava and I even caught him blushing one time when Bailey sat really close to him at the fire pit and her hair sort of rubbed against his bare shoulder.

Obviously, I was a little jealous that Brennan seemed more into her than he was into me. But I'd promised the girls I wouldn't do anything to sabotage whatever Bailey had going, and these weren't the kind of girls I wanted to go back on my word with. It was weird, feeling so *loyal* to someone, but I guess maybe that's what a month at the lake does to people?

My dad seemed pleased that I was getting out and "making the most of things," as he put it. My mom, on the other hand? Well, she still wasn't enjoying herself at all. But the good thing about having friends to hang out with during the day was, I could mostly avoid her. And I hardly even noticed that she still had my phone! Without my friends texting to remind me how much fun they were having without me, I was free to admit that I was having fun without them (and I didn't even miss their text messages, which had mostly just been them making fun of the fact that I was in the middle of nowhere with a bunch of nobodies).

One day, after the adults had finished up with their day's creative sessions, Bailey's mom suggested we all have an impromptu picnic. "Let's do it at the jumping rock!" Bailey said. The jumping rock was really just a small, rocky island out in the middle of the lake with a seriously deep drop off on one side. I'd never been out there, but I'd heard everyone else talking about it.

After we all returned to our cabins to gather whatever snack food we could scrounge up, almost everyone—except my mom, who had a million excuses for why she had to stay back—piled into the canoes that were lined up along the shoreline. We started the short paddle out to the little island in the middle of the lake.

"Gorgeous," my dad mused as we struggled to keep up with everyone else. I could feel the canoe listing to the side as he dug deeply into the water. He was obviously trying to look like a canoe pro but probably just looked like he was exerting a ridiculous amount of energy for a relaxing evening boat ride.

"It is pretty," I agreed. It really wasn't worth getting embarrassed about my dad's dorky behavior, since I knew no one cared. We all had parents at this retreat, and they'd all done something totally embarrassing at some point while we were there. It was nice spending a little time with Dad, even if he was still in work mode and totally obsessing over his image.

"I hope you're not totally miserable," Dad said, grunting as he attempted to steer us to the right. We kept veering way left, then way right, instead. I just kept paddling in my seat at the front of the canoe, and tried to stay as calm as possible. I still had a tiny problem with tipping canoes when I was in them, so my dad and I weren't exactly the smoothest pair.

I shook my head, but realized he was probably staring out at his paddle instead of my head. "I'm having an okay time, actually," I said aloud, and meant it. "Bailey and Ava are great. And everyone else, too. It's definitely not as bad as I thought it would be."

"The other girls seem chill," he said, and I rolled my eyes. That was my dad—super-cheesy but trying to play it cool in front of all the others. Not that anyone could hear us, since we'd fallen *way* behind, but still.

"Yep," I said, giggling. "Chill."

Dad chuckled, then he said, "I'm glad you came along. And I really appreciate you making an effort, Izzy." I shrugged, and that was the end of the conversation.

When we finally got to the island, I was surprised to see that Bailey's mom had already set up a bunch of huge picnic blankets. The adults were all congregating on a big hill with a view of the resort back onshore. Bailey's mom had brought enough sandwich stuff for everyone, which was incredibly generous.

I guess Bailey saw me staring at the impressive picnic spread. She leaned over to whisper, "Last year, Mom decided to try to *make* sandwiches for everyone one night, to thank people for coming to the retreat—but she forgot to put anything inside a few of them, and a couple people just got plain pieces of bread. So this year, it's a serve-yourself sandwich bar."

I laughed. "At least she tried." I thought about my mom, who was still grumping around our cabin by herself, instead of making the most of things. "That's worth something."

"She *always* tries," Bailey said, laughing. "You should have seen my school lunches when I was in elementary school. Sometimes I'd get two sandwiches, and other days, I'd get nothing but carrot sticks. Obviously, I make my own lunch now so I don't starve."

"Prepare for launch!" Bailey and I heard Levi holler as we wandered away from the adults and crested the rocky hill to where our friends were hanging out. Ava and Brennan and everyone had settled on the other side of the island, as far from the parents as we could all get. After a few weeks of togetherness, the resort was starting to feel really small. So whenever we could physically separate ourselves from the adults, we did.

"In three, two . . ." Levi held up one finger and mouthed a silent *one*, then jumped off the edge of the rock. He plummeted at least ten feet before hitting the surface of the water.

I peeked over the edge to make sure he was still alive. Levi popped up out of the water with a huge grin on his face. "Survival! The jumping champion! Rahhhh . . . roahhhh!" He made fake crowd sounds, even though none of us were actually cheering for him. Levi was sort of a strange guy—but he was always entertaining.

"Oh . . ." Ava moaned on the ground next to me and put her head between her knees.

"You okay?" I asked. I plunked down next to her as Brennan and Zach leapt off the top of the rocks. Bailey followed close behind them, screeching as she sailed through the air. I could hear them all splash as they hit the water below. Madeline, who'd climbed down to a lower rock shelf, jumped in after them. Ava whimpered. "You sound like Coco," I said, nudging her.

Ava looked at me through her bangs, then hung her head between her legs again. "Thanks a lot."

"What's wrong?"

"The jumping rock always freaks me out," she said. "Stupid, I know."

"Not stupid," I said.

"I *want* to jump off, but every time I get anywhere close to the edge, I panic."

"So don't jump," I said.

"Not an option," Ava said. "If I skipped out on all the things that scared me, I'd be the most boring person on earth."

"What else scares you?" I asked, trying to distract her.

"Heights, bugs, getting up in front of a group of people . . . the list goes on and on." Ava sat up and tilted her face toward the sun.

I scooted across the rock and peered down over the edge of the drop-off again. It looked super-fun. But then again, I wasn't afraid of heights. I scooted back up to my spot beside Ava.

Brennan and Madeline both climbed up the side of the rock and shook their hair like shaggy dogs. Water droplets flew through the air, soaking us. Levi suddenly appeared with a huge water bottle full of lake water, and shook it out on our heads. Ava and I both jumped up and ran.

"You can run, but you can't hide from the Lake Monster!" Levi said in a strange, low voice. "Hello, hello, we have come to slime you."

"Sometimes I wonder what it's like being inside Levi's mind," Ava whispered, as we crouched behind a tree. We both laughed, then ran again as Zach crept over and tried to toss a wet towel over our heads.

"If I held your hand," I said to Ava, "and you closed your eyes . . . do you think you could jump? If we soak ourselves, they're going to leave us alone, right?"

Ava's eyes opened wide, and she began to moan again. Just as she started to sink down onto the ground, Bailey and Brennan snuck up behind us with armloads full of wet leaves that they'd gathered from somewhere. The leaves were slimy and disgusting, and I knew there were probably dozens of dead bugs hiding inside the pile of yuck.

I screamed and shook them off myself as Ava did the same. Bailey and Brennan leaned against each other and laughed, like they'd never seen anything so hilarious in their lives.

"You're going to pay," I said, pulling leaves out of Ava's hair. "You'll regret this. . . ." I narrowed my eyes and made a fierce fighter look.

"Ooh," Brennan said in his arrogant, mocking tone. He

and Bailey were both still laughing, which made it impossible for me not to smile a little bit, too. They were just so cute together! "I'm so scared—tough-guy Izzy is going to get us, Bailey. Run!" He wiggled his arms in the air like a cartoon alien, trying to get us to laugh.

Suddenly, Ava grabbed my hand. "I'm closing my eyes," she said. "I trust you."

I looked over and saw that she was telling the truth. Her eyes were squeezed closed, and she had a determined look on her face. I led her toward the edge of the rock. As we walked forward, I held up my hand to make sure everyone backed off and left us alone for a few seconds. They did.

Moments later, Ava and I were at the edge of the jumping rock. "Ready?"

Ava just grunted.

"You don't have to do this, you know," I said. "No one cares if you jump or don't jump. We can climb down the path and just walk into the water instead."

Ava gritted her teeth and growled, "I care."

I shrugged, even though she couldn't see me. "Okay. On three."

"Izzy?" Ava said, opening her eyes just a crack to squint at me.

"Yeah?"

"Hold my hand the whole time, and pull me hard so I jump out far enough, okay?"

I smiled, then she closed her eyes again. "One . . . ," I said, looking over my shoulder to find that Levi, Brennan, Zach, Bailey, and Madeline were all watching us quietly. "Two . . ." Ava gripped my hand harder, so I squeezed back. "Three."

As I crouched down to jump, I glanced over and saw that Ava's eyes were wide open. She looked back at me, smiled, then we both jumped. Seconds later, we hit the water. It felt like we were sinking forever. Bubbles were everywhere, then suddenly we were back up at the top of the water.

"I did it!" Ava cried happily as we bobbed on the surface. "I finally did it!"

"You did it." As we swam toward the tiny shore that would lead us to the path back up to the top of the rock, the others cheered above us.

When we climbed up again, everyone jumped again and again, until our legs were sore and we were starving. After dinner, my friends and I all found a spot to lie down on the warm rocks. Bailey squeezed in next to Brennan, while I shared a towel with Ava. Madeline and Zach had brought

UNO cards, and they played game after game—losing only a few cards to the wind. Levi whittled nearby, then built a tiny fire in a crack in the rocks.

We lay around until the sun went down, laughing and talking like we'd been friends for years.

Chapter Eleven

Do you guys want to sleep at my cabin tonight?" Ava asked as we devoured roasted marshmallows by the fire one night.

"Yes!" Bailey said, in her usual loud voice. "It's so cramped in our cabin. Mom is starting to drive me crazy."

"*Your* mom is?" I said. "My mom was literally standing in the door of my room this morning, just staring at me when I woke up." I laughed, but couldn't shake the feeling of how creepy it was when I woke up and found my mom watching me. It was almost as though she thought I was capable of doing something wrong in my sleep. When I sat up and told her she was freaking me out, she told me my hair looked sun-damaged. Nice.

"I'll have to check with my mom," Bailey said, "but I'm sure it will be fine."

"Yeah," I said, even though I hadn't really *asked* my parents' permission in a while. Usually, I just told them what I was going to do—spending the night at Heidi's, shopping with Sylvie, whatever. They hadn't really put a foot down until we started to discuss the month at the lake, and then they suddenly adopted all this parental control. If Bailey was going to ask, I realized there was no harm in me asking politely too.

I'd noticed that since I'd started hanging out with Bailey and Ava during the day, my mom and I had been getting along a little better. Maybe—*maybe*—it had something to do with my change in attitude and the fact that we weren't walking all over each other all day. Or maybe she was just getting used to the woods. Whatever it was, it was kind of nice. "I'll check with mine, too."

"Yay!" Ava squeaked.

A few minutes later, Bailey and I both stood on the front stoop of Ava's cabin with blankets tucked under our arms. Coco sat by my side, looking up at Ava hopefully.

"Ooh, good, I was hoping you'd bring Coco. She'll keep Madeline occupied!" She reached down to pat my puppy, then waved us in. "Come on in. My dad promised he'd stay out of the way. He and Madeline went out for a moonlight canoe ride so we can have the cabin to ourselves for a while."

We set up our makeshift beds in the living room, since Ava had promised her sister she could keep the bedroom for the night. "I hate sleeping on hard surfaces," I admitted as I layered blankets thick on the floor. "I'm kind of a nature wimp."

"Oh, I was the exact same way our first summer here too," Ava said, nodding. "Every single bug bite made me cry and hide inside. And then one night, a raccoon showed up at the campfire and I completely freaked out." She and Bailey both started laughing hysterically. Ava snorted so hard she got the hiccups, which just made them both laugh even harder.

Finally, Bailey stopped laughing long enough to tell more of the story. "Ava stood up on one of the benches by the campfire and started jumping up and down. She was screaming and yelping and pointing at the raccoon, but she couldn't even say anything because she just kept screaming. We were all so busy staring at Ava that no one saw the raccoon hiding in the bushes. So we thought she'd made the whole thing up—"

Ava cut her off. "Until the next night, when the raccoon came *again*! Bailey turned around to get a stick for her marshmallow, and there it was, standing in the shadows, just staring at her. Like, *right* behind her."

Bailey grinned. "I was totally composed, unlike Ava."

"You were not!" Ava argued, swatting at her with a pillow. "You screamed even louder than I did. And maybe you should tell Izzy who eventually scared it away?"

"You?" I asked, looking at Ava.

"Me," she said, grinning. "I grabbed one of Levi's whittled sticks and pointed it right at that freaky thing, like a sword. I don't think I scared it very much, since it just sort of waddled away, but I did save Bailey from rabies." She peeked at us from under her bangs. "Maybe."

"I owe you my life," Bailey said, then crawled over to hug Ava. They both dissolved into a fit of giggles again.

Watching the way Bailey and Ava interacted with each other made me really oddly happy. They teased each other, but not in a way that was meant to be hurtful. They were both sarcastic, but not to the point of cruelty. And I had a feeling that when they said something, they actually meant it. The best thing of all was, I never wondered if they were talking about me behind my back, and I never worried that they were faking happiness when they were really bored or annoyed.

With Heidi and Sylvie, I worried about all of those things.

"Do you want to play Liar and Spy?" Bailey asked, shaking me out of my own head.

"What's that?" I was intrigued.

"Ooh, ooh!" Ava started bouncing up and down. Coco, who'd made herself comfortable at the foot of Ava's floor bed, shifted and whined in her sleep. Ava bent down and whispered, "Sorry, Coco."

Bailey explained, "In Liar and Spy, you get to decide if you want to do a spy mission—which we will design for you—or if you want us to figure out if you're a liar. You make three statements—things about yourself, usually—and we have to figure out if you're telling the truth or making stuff up."

"Basically," Ava said, "It's like Truth or Dare—but not." She was giving me a funny look. "What? Does it sound dumb?" She flushed, her cheeks turning bright red behind her hair.

I realized I'd been giving them a weird look. "No," I said quickly. "It doesn't sound dumb."

"We don't have to do it," Ava said quietly. "It was just an idea."

"Who goes first? I can, if you want," I said, realizing I was going to have to make it really obvious that I was psyched about the idea. Even though we'd been spending a lot of time together, there were still times when Bailey and Ava were sort of cautious around me, almost like I was a wild animal that might snap at a moment's notice. In fairness, that's exactly what I was like in school, but I was a whole different person in the middle of the woods.

"I'll go first, since you haven't played before. Okay?" Bailey said. She didn't wait for me to say okay, just charged on. "I'm going to do Liar. So I'll say three things, and you guys have to figure out if I'm lying."

Ava and I settled back on our blankets, waiting while Bailey stood up and cleared her throat. "First truth . . . *or is it a lie?*" she said loudly, lifting one eyebrow. "I hate wearing skirts. One hundred percent, total loathing, despise skirts. Some people look okay in them—Izzy looks cute—but I look like I stole my mom's clothes and tried to pull them off as my own."

"That's the truth," Ava whispered to me.

"I probably would have guessed that," I whispered back. "She's worn the same tank top and cutoff shorts since the first day we got here." As soon as I said it, I realized my comment sounded judgmental. It wasn't meant to be. It was just a statement of fact. But I knew I had to be careful not to sound like the snob I sometimes was. "Not that there's anything wrong with that," I added, just to make sure Ava didn't think I was criticizing Bailey's clothes.

"Second," Bailey said. She paused to think. "I have a

major, major crush on Brennan, and am having a seriously hard time hanging out with him without freaking out every second. He had this piece of melty marshmallow stuck to his upper lip when we were making s'mores at the bonfire the other night, and I literally almost licked it off him. Then I realized it would have totally creeped him out, having this random girl in a dirty tank top lick his face like a dog. So I backed off. Can you imagine? If I'd actually licked him, I mean?"

Ava and I both laughed. "That one is totally obvious," Ava said.

"Truth!" I said. "I really hope you come up with something better for the last one. So far yours are way too easy!"

Bailey narrowed her eyes and said, "Okay, try this one: I was a surprise."

"What do you mean, 'a surprise'?" Ava asked, pushing her hair away from her face. I'd come to find it sort of charming, the way Ava's hair always slipped down over her face. While we were dancing one day, little pieces kept flying all over the place in front of her eyes and into her mouth. That's when she told me how she'd been trying to grow her bangs out for more than a year, but she'd made the critical error of trying to trim and shape them herself between cuts. Now, her hair fell over her eyes all the time and no matter what she did, it refused to cooperate. I had loaned her one of my headbands, but she always forgot to wear it. She said it was a little stupid to accessorize at the lake, and I had to agree.

Bailey shrugged. "My parents were done having kids. I guess they only ever wanted one, and they had my perfect brother, and then—*surprise!*—four years later, Mom found out she was pregnant with me." Bailey smiled smugly at us. "Do I tell the truth, or am I lying?"

Ava and I looked at each other. "I think that's a lie," I said. "There's no way your mom would have *told you* you were a surprise, even if it was the truth. It's like she was telling you you were an accident, and that's kind of awful."

"Aha!" Bailey said, pointing her finger in the air. "It's the truth! I was one hundred percent surprise. Surprise kid number two. *Moi!*"

"How did that even come up in casual conversation?" I asked, incredulous. "You were just sitting around the breakfast table one day, and your mom said, 'Hey, Bailey, pass the Cheerios, and by the way, we never wanted a second kid—you were a huge surprise. La-di-da, let's all have some hot chocolate and celebrate'?"

Bailey laughed. "No, it wasn't like that! I can't even

remember how it came up, actually. But my mom and I are pretty honest with each other, so I guess she just must have told me sometime."

I shook my head, still in shock that Bailey was being so casual about it. Maybe it seemed crazy to me, because I knew if my mom had told me something like that, it would have come across in a totally nasty way. She would have saved it up for the middle of some war, when she really wanted to hit me hard. She would *not* have been able to say it in a mother-daughter-bonding, we-all-love-each-other-now sort of way. "My mom and I are pretty honest with each other too," I said. "But in our house, 'honest' just means we totally slam each other and she snaps at me all the time."

Bailey frowned. "It really wasn't a big deal. It didn't hurt my feelings or anything, since my mom was really nice about it all. Mom kind of goes overboard reassuring me that I'm *very* wanted now, so I don't feel less loved or something. Apparently, as soon as she saw my feet on an ultrasound she was convinced I was a good idea." She held one of her feet in the air and wiggled her toes. "I do have very nice feet."

"You do," I agreed, then reached out and tickled the bottom of her foot. She was so ticklish that she actually fell over, and soon we were all in the middle of a huge tickle fight in the pile of blankets. Of course, that's when Madeline and Ava's dad came back from their canoe ride.

We all tried to stop laughing, but for some reason it was impossible. As Madeline and her dad snuck past, staring at us like we were crazy people, we dissolved into a fit of giggles again.

Chapter Twelve

A n hour later, we were still playing Liar and Spy. While we talked, I gave Ava and Bailey manicures and pedicures. When I finished their nails (and also Madeline's, who promised Ava she'd leave us alone if we let her hang out for a little while), Ava did my toes and Bailey painted my hands. "You're the worst nail painter ever," I told Bailey. "I think my fingers have more polish on them than my finger-nails do."

"I just do things differently," she said, laughing as she slapped the brush against my fingers. The way she painted nails almost reminded me of the way a modern artist would flick a brush at a canvas. She held my hands out in front of her and studied her work. "I think it looks beautiful," she said.

"Um . . . ," I said. "It's definitely creative. Maybe not something I'd pay for, but . . ." I giggled. Each of my nails was a different color, and the polish was messy and glopped on. But at least they were my real nails, grown in and healthy-looking. Since I'd started hanging out with Bailey and Ava, I'd stopped picking at my nails. I guess I was just more relaxed or something, but I didn't seem to have much nervous energy at the lake. So even though they didn't look perfect—or even pretty—they looked sort of healthy and fun. And they reminded me of an awesome night.

Most of the time that night, we were laughing hilariously about someone's seriously funny or seriously stupid secrets— but sometimes the truth someone shared was also sort of sad.

I'd discovered that, when she was seven, Bailey had thrown up in the pool at swimming lessons (yuck!). In keeping with the pool theme, she also told us that when he was eight, her brother pooped at the bottom of the pool during swim team practice, thinking it would be funny (super-yuck!).

Then Ava told us about how her stepfather kept a snake in his bedroom that only ate live mice (um, cool?). We also found out that one time she made and ate an entire tube of Halloween slice-and-bake cookies in one night and felt so sick afterward that she hadn't eaten them since.

I admitted that I once stole a poster of a cute puppy sitting on a dictionary that was hanging up in the school library (pitiful). And neither of them believed me when I told them that my dad had once toilet-papered his *own* house, just so people would think he was popular (I guess TP-ing was a sign of coolness or something in the town where he grew up).

After Madeline went to bed—with Coco trotting along happily behind her—I reluctantly confessed that I'd once let Jake Theisen read a note that Heidi had given me where she talked about how hot he was. "Why?" Ava asked, without any judgment. "Why would you do that to a friend?"

"I don't know," I said, realizing that I really *didn't* know. I guess it had just seemed funny at the time, but Heidi was crushed when she found out. "I wish I hadn't."

I also admitted that I'd been lying to everyone about dance tryouts. "Soccer doesn't really get in the way at all—practice is on different days, which everyone will eventually figure out. I just don't want to humiliate myself in front of the whole school by trying out. Sometimes," I confessed, "I worry about looking stupid."

I thought this was a very profound statement, but Bailey and Ava both laughed. "What?" I demanded. "What's funny about that?"

"Um," Bailey mumbled through a mouthful of Oreo cookie, "you and everyone else. Do you think you're the only person in the history of seventh grade that's worried about her reputation?"

I held out my hand for a cookie and shook my head. "No, it's just—I don't know. I feel like I have more to lose if I really embarrass myself."

"That is so self-centered," Ava said, lifting her eyebrows. She rarely put things so bluntly, so it caught me off guard. My cookie tasted like cardboard in my mouth, and I kind of wanted to spit it out.

Bailey nodded. "You're more popular than ninety-nine percent of our class, but that doesn't mean it's a bigger deal when you do something stupid. It's just a bigger deal to *you*."

"But it *is* a bigger deal," I pressed on, though my face was getting hot, and I was a little queasy. I hated when Bailey and Ava confronted me about saying selfish things. They didn't understand what it was like for me, how it felt like everyone was always watching me, waiting for me to screw up, just so they could laugh at me. It was like I was more visible than most people at school. Most of the time, I liked it that way, but sometimes I felt like I had to be extra cautious. "I just mean, when I do something that makes me look stupid, it seems like the whole school is watching."

"They're not," Ava said. "You just think they are."

"But they are," I argued. "If I did something completely embarrassing—like fall on my face during dance tryouts—everyone in school would know about it."

"Yeah," Bailey admitted. "I guess you have a point. But the thing is, if you just laughed it off, you could probably make people forget about it in two days. If one of *us* humiliated ourselves in front of the whole school, it would probably get blown up into this huge deal and whatever it was would follow us around until we graduated from high school. Like Susannah Green! Everyone called her Crybaby Green all last year because someone spread a rumor that she started crying about missing her favorite stuffed animal during Spanish. Remember that?"

The look on my face must have made it obvious that *I* was the one who had spread around the rumor about Susannah. She really had cried about something stupid and babyish, like missing her stuffed animal. I think. I wasn't actually in the same class with her when it happened, but Heidi had given me the details and, of course, we'd laughed about it all week.

Who does that in sixth grade? Susannah really hadn't

lived it down, but I'd never really thought about it much after that day. It didn't affect me on a daily basis, so I'd never really considered that the story had never gone away. It trailed her all year. Because of me. "Wow," I said finally. "Poor Susannah."

"Yeah," Bailey sighed. "The thing you maybe don't realize is, most people care a lot less about what you and your friends are doing all the time than I bet you think they do. Mostly, I think people just kind of try to stay out of your way and hope you don't even notice them."

I began to pick at my pinkie nail for the first time in over a week. Bailey saw me and said, "Hey! You're going to ruin my hard work."

"Oh," I said, stuffing my hands under my thighs. "Sorry." After a moment's pause, I said, "Do *you* guys avoid me at school?"

"Pretty much, yeah," Bailey said, smiling sheepishly. "But it's a whole different world here at the lake, isn't it?"

I nodded. "Yeah. And you guys are so different than I thought you would be."

"At first," Ava said quietly, "you were exactly like I thought you would be. But now, you're different."

"I'm really glad you guys ended up being here with me

this summer," I said. "I don't think I would have survived without someone other than my parents to talk to this whole month." All night, I'd been surprised at how much I was telling these newish friends. But at the same time, it was such a relief to confess some of my real feelings and fears to someone and know that the truth wouldn't come back to haunt me.

Because I knew my secrets were safe with Bailey and Ava, I also told them about my relationship with my parents and how much my dad had changed over the last two or three years. I'd complained about my annoying and critical parents with Heidi and Sylvie, of course, but I'd never admitted that my relationship with my mom and dad made me feel sad sometimes. I felt sort of wimpy, somehow, admitting that I was bummed because my dad never wanted to take me for ice cream anymore—that just sounded like a preschool problem. But I had a feeling Ava and Bailey might understand that it hurt to be forgotten by your parents. That sometimes I wanted to be noticed for more than my bad habits and worse attitude.

"My dad and I used to be really close," I said. "But then, it was almost as if one day, he decided I was just this obstacle that moves around the house and gets in the way. We used to hang out on the weekends, avoiding my mom together, but now I feel like we're all avoiding each other at the same time."

"Why would you avoid your mom?" Ava asked. She'd told us, earlier in the night, about how her dad had ended up getting primary custody of her and Madeline when her parents divorced. Apparently, he had a more flexible job, and her mom travels all the time—so it worked out better for everyone for them to live with their dad most of the time. But I could tell Ava missed having her mom at home and missed having her around for a lot of regular life and girly stuff.

"She's really critical, and we just don't get along," I said. "She's not the warmest person on earth."

"I don't think I've even said a single word to her in the three weeks we've been here," Bailey said, pulling her eyebrows together. "She hardly ever comes to the bonfires at night, does she?"

"Nope. She's sort of afraid of people."

"Is she really?" Ava asked. "Like she has a phobia or something?"

"No," I said, laughing at how serious Ava looked. She looked worried, as though my mom suffered from some sort of chronic problem, instead of just major stranger issues and general crankiness. "Not like that. She's just sort of snobby, I guess." But then I realized it wasn't snootiness; it was something else. Something that I myself had felt in the first few days at the lake. "Actually, it's not that she's snobby, but I think she's maybe afraid she won't really know what to say to people she doesn't know that well. She's not great at just chatting with strangers, so sometimes she comes across as unfriendly or sort of bossy and harsh."

"*Is* she unfriendly?" Bailey asked.

"More shy than anything, probably," I said, shrugging. "I guess I've never really thought about it all that much. But I think it's in situations like this, where she doesn't really know anyone at all, that she's super-bad at faking it. So she's been a total grump all month, and my dad has been so consumed with work that I don't even really know why he forced us to come with him. Except for the night we all went on that picnic, I've hardly even seen him."

I took a deep breath. I was really annoyed, all of a sudden. "I think my dad would have been a lot happier this month if he'd just come alone. Then he wouldn't have to worry about my mom and me screwing up his 'reputation.'" I made quotation marks in the air, since that's what I'd heard him say to my mom when he was giving her a hard time about her rarely showing up for the evening activities. I think my dad was getting pretty frustrated with my mom's bad attitude at the lake too. So maybe he and I still had something in common.

"Do you ever tell your parents how you're feeling?" Bailey asked, her eyes wide and innocent.

"Ha." I laughed bitterly, thinking about all the times I'd told my parents how I was feeling and how well *that* had gone over. "They don't really care for my honesty. The whole sharing-our-feelings thing doesn't really happen in our house." Then I thought about it for a second, and realized that most of the time, me sharing my feelings meant me talking back. I hadn't told my dad that I missed our ice-cream outings, or that sometimes it would be nice to *talk* to him instead of formally *communicating* with him.

Suddenly, I didn't want to talk about it anymore, since I was getting bummed out after a night full of fun. So I waved my hands in the air and said, "Let's stop talking about my defective relationship with my parents and move on to something more interesting. Do you guys realize we've only played half of our game? No one has done Spy yet. The game is Liar *and* Spy, right?"

Bailey yawned. "Yeah, but what are we supposed to spy

on? It's pitch-black out there, and remember, the friendly raccoons are out now."

"True," I said. "I forgot about the raccoons."

"But would it be worth risking a run-in with the raccoons . . . ," Ava said, rubbing her hands together, "if we spied on Brennan?"

Chapter Thirteen

We had to sneak out of the cabin very quietly. Not because of Ava's dad, who apparently wore earplugs at night (the sound of the crickets chirping in the woods kept him from falling asleep), but because I knew Coco was a super-light sleeper, and my trusty puppy would totally give us away if she thought we were going out on an adventure without her. She was probably curled up, fast asleep, on Madeline's pillow, but we didn't want to risk it. So we all tiptoed out the screen door and down the front steps of the cabin.

The moon was nearly full, so the pathways were somewhat visible in a smattering of places. But the trees hung low in other sections of the path, choking out any kind of light at all. "This is really creepy," I whispered as we picked our way toward the clearing that housed the communal fire pit area. There, the trees opened up into a big circle where the moon could shine through. Brennan's family's cabin was down a long path on the other side of the fire pit. About as far away from Ava's cabin as you could possibly get.

"Abort mission?" Bailey suggested, when we were only about ten feet away from Ava's front steps. "More lies and truths instead?"

"No way," Ava said, leading us down the path. "Let's see what Bren looks like when he's asleep. I wonder if he snores."

I giggled quietly. "What if he sleeps with a blankie?"

"I really hope he does," Ava said, laughing along with me. "That would make this mission totally worth it."

We stopped when we reached the fire pit. "It's that path, right?" Ava asked, pointing into the darkness. "Or that one?"

In the dark, everything looked totally different than it did during the day. I could see the Cardinal cabin from one of the benches that surrounded the campfire. It was dark inside, so my parents were obviously asleep. I wasn't even quite sure what time it was—probably close to midnight.

"It's that one," Bailey said certainly. "But I'm not going first. It's really dark." The sound of a stick cracking nearby made us all jump and huddle together. "What was that?"

"Just a squirrel, probably," Ava said, but she didn't sound very sure of herself. "Or a raccoon, coming to get you." She held her hands in the air like claws and wiggled them in Bailey's face. Bailey yelped.

We stuck even closer to each other as we walked toward the path to Brennan's cabin. I grabbed Bailey's hand and tugged her along behind me as we stepped onto the wooded path. "Why are we doing this?" Bailey whispered.

"Because it's fun," Ava said. She turned back to look at us, her face barely illuminated by the moonlight. Leaves cast long shadows on her skin, making her look sort of spotted. She reminded me of a pony, all skinny limbs and wild hair and wide eyes.

We crept down the path, almost tiptoeing because we were stepping so carefully. Periodically, one of our feet would land off the edge of the path just the littlest bit. Brush snapped and crinkled under our weight, sounding like a wild animal was walking alongside us in the woods. "I jump every single time someone does that," Bailey said when my foot acciden-tally landed in a pile of dried-up leaves.

When we had Brennan's cabin in our sights, Ava stopped. We stood in a little open area on the path, where there was just enough moonlight that we could see each other. If anyone was looking out of the window of Brennan's cabin, they could *also* see us. I decided not to mention that to anyone, since I figured we all sort of realized the risks that came with our mission.

"Now what?" Ava asked, her hands on her hips. Her eyes were fixed on Brennan's cabin.

"Now we peek in the windows," I said, trying to sound more confident than I felt. "Anyone know which room is his?"

"What we're doing is slightly psychopath-ish. You guys know that, right?" Bailey asked. She twisted her hair up into a loose bun and jabbed a stick in it to keep it in place. "If we get caught, I'm the one that's going to look especially insane. He already thinks I'm obsessed with him."

"How do you do that?" I asked, pointing at her hair to try to distract her. Bailey was always twisting her hair up and keeping it off her neck using sticks, a pencil, a fork—she could get her curly hair to do just about anything she wanted it to do. It was pretty impressive.

"I just twist and stick," said Bailey, with a flip of her hands. "My hair gets kind of gross sometimes if I tie it up with sticks, but who really cares when you're in the middle of nowhere, right?"

"It looks pretty when you have it all piled up like that," I said.

"Yeah, yeah," Ava said, turning away from Brennan's cabin to look at both of us. "Enough stalling. Bailey looks like a Greek goddess in the pale glow of the moon with her hair just so. We get it."

We all laughed because Ava was acting so un-Ava-like and the whole situation was totally ridiculous.

There were no lights on in Brennan's cabin, which made the spying a lot less intimidating. If they'd been up, reading or playing games or whatever their family did at night, it would be really awkward. Not that what we were doing *wasn't* awkward just because it was dark, but knowing we probably wouldn't get caught definitely helped a little. Ava crept up the front steps and peered into the living room window. "Oy," she stage-whispered. "Get your butts over here."

Bailey wrapped her arm through mine, and together we snuck up the steps to join Ava. "There's no one in there," I said, pressing my face against the glass.

"I know," Ava whispered. She pointed to the back of the cabin. "Bedrooms."

"Okay . . . ," Bailey murmured. "But what if they sleep naked or something?"

"That's what we're here to find out, right?" I said quietly as we tiptoed back down the creaky stairs. "It's a spy mission. We need to gather some recon." I paused at the bottom of the stairs. "Wait. Do you sleep naked, Bailey? Is that, like, a common thing?"

"No!" she said, rather loudly, given the circumstances. "But I know some people do." She twisted a curl that had escaped from the pile of hair on top of her head—it was now snaking down her neck. "I don't want to know if Brennan is one of those people."

"There's, like, a two percent chance that he is," Ava whispered. Her voice was very matter-of-fact. "But we could find out, if you two would quit stalling!"

Bailey and I grinned at each other. I was pretty sure we were both thinking the same thing—that Ava was a different person when she was on a spy mission. Like, her usual shy-girl attitude was just a daytime cover-up for some scandalous nighttime secret identity.

We skimmed under the branches that pressed up against the sides of the cabin and made our way to the back of the Snowy Owl cabin. There were only two windows at the back of the building—one for each bedroom. The tree cover was so dense that there was almost no light around back, so I couldn't see Bailey's or Ava's facial expressions. We all just looked like dark blobs under the trees. I could hear Bailey's ragged breathing—it made me worry she was going to have a panic attack.

"Who wants to peek first?" I asked, hoping Ava would volunteer. She seemed eager.

But instead, she said, "Not me. I did all the hard work up until now. One of you has to go first this time."

"Don't you feel like we're, like, violating their privacy or something?" Bailey asked, after a few seconds of silence.

"Fine," Ava said with a huff. "I'll look first. You are the biggest wimp."

Something about the way she said it made me start laughing—hard. Unfortunately, that got Bailey going, and suddenly, we were all cracking up outside what was very possibly Brennan's bedroom window. Bailey began to snort, which sent Ava into total hysterics. We were no longer quiet and stealthy. Instead, we sounded like a pack of yipping hyenas.

The light flicked on, on the other side of the glass, and seconds later, a face peered out into the darkness. It was Brennan. "Aah!" Ava yelped.

Bailey threw herself to the ground, howling with laughter. I pulled her up, then dragged her around to the side of the house. Because it was so dark out, I was pretty sure Brennan hadn't actually seen us—but there was no doubt that he had *heard* us. Embarrassed and freaked out, we ran, tripping on sticks as we all barreled back down the path to the fire pit.

"That is so embarrassing," Bailey hissed as the full realization of what had just happened hit us. We'd been caught snooping at Brennan's window in the middle of the night. "Oh. Oh no. Oh my God, I'm so embarrassed."

"Did anyone, by any chance, see what he was wearing?" Ava asked, giggling. "Was he wearing cute jammies?"

This made us all laugh even harder.

"Let's go down by the lake, where at least no one can hear us, okay?" Bailey said when we had all calmed down just a little bit. "What if his parents heard us laughing and woke up, and now they're out searching for us?"

I giggled. "I think that's highly unlikely. For one thing, it's the middle of the night and it was pretty obvious that the three giggly people outside Brennan's window weren't mass murderers lurking around, waiting to pounce."

"So you think he knew it was us?" Bailey asked, cringing.

"Um, yes," Ava nodded. She glanced at me, and we both started laughing again.

The path to the lake was better lit than the paths to the

cabins were. The moon guided us down to the beach area. We sat at the end of the dock and dangled our feet in the water. "Do we need to attempt another spy mission, since that one was a total bust?" I asked, poking my toes up to wiggle them on the surface of the lake.

"I don't think we're cut out for this business," Ava said matter-of-factly. "I mean, I think I might be decent at it, but with sidekicks like you two, I'm sort of doomed."

"We could toilet-paper Izzy's cabin," Bailey suggested, after a long silence. "I bet her dad would like that. Maybe he'd think it was, like, some sort of new-guy initiation thing."

I laughed. "I'm sure I'd be stuck cleaning it up," I said. "My mom would probably make me actually *use* the toilet paper I pulled out of the trees as punishment or something."

"That's disgusting," Ava said.

"Yeah," I agreed. "Maybe we should just go swimming instead? Raccoons don't swim, do they?"

"I think we're safe in the water," Bailey said.

"Night swimming," Ava said happily. "Sounds perfect."

And it was.

Chapter Fourteen

~~~~~~~~~~~~~~~~

We all knew summer would end, of course. It had to. But none of us really talked about what would happen next, or how our friendship might have to change now that we were returning home. I knew things would be different, but I hoped we could maintain something of what we'd developed over the summer. I'd grown really close to both Ava and Bailey, and I wasn't willing to just walk away from our new friendship.

But the thing that kept bothering me was, I didn't know what would happen when seventh grade started. I wasn't sure how Bailey and Ava would fit into my world back home. They were great summer friends, but I didn't know if they could really be *forever* friends. What would Heidi and Sylvie think if I suddenly started hanging out with these girls we'd teased so much in our first year of middle school? I knew my home friends would probably hate both my summer friends, the way that I had when I'd first arrived at the lake.

"I guess I'll see you next week," Bailey said, as she helped her mom pack the rest of their things into their car. My family had been slow to get going, since my mom felt it was her job to clean every last nook and cranny of our cabin before we could leave. I guess it was a decent thing to do, but seemed a little like overkill. My dad and I just let her go at it while we hung around outside, saying good-bye to everyone else and taking one last swim.

"Yeah," I said, letting Bailey pull me into a hug. "See you next week."

"It's going to be different when we get back, huh?" She was still hugging me when she said this, so I couldn't see what kind of expression was on her face.

"Definitely different," I agreed. I don't know why I didn't say something at that moment to reassure Bailey—and myself—that our relationship at school *would* be different, now that we'd spent part of the summer together. I should have told her that I wanted to try to find a way to have our friendship work when we returned home. But I couldn't say

137

it. Because I wasn't sure it would work. I felt like something about me had changed in the month I'd spent with Bailey and Ava, but I wasn't sure if it would *stay* changed when we got back home. Things didn't usually work like that.

Bailey stepped out of our hug and nodded. "Well. See ya."

Ava came bounding over and pulled both of us into one of her tiny hugs. "Good luck with dance tryouts next week!" I said, squeezing her close. "You're going to be amazing."

She smiled at me. "I hope so. Thanks, Izzy. And I know it's super-dorky for me to say it out loud, but I just wanted to tell you it was really fun getting to know you this summer."

"You too," I agreed. "Both of you. I had the best summer ever." I was about to go on, to tell them that I'd look for them in the hall. Or that maybe we could have lunch together one day. Or maybe, one night, they could come over for a sleepover at my house. But before I could say anything, Bailey screeched and the moment had passed.

"Oh! Oh!" she said, digging for something in her pocket. "Look what Brennan gave me just before he left." She couldn't even wait for us to open the piece of paper to see what was inside. She blurted out, "His phone number! He told me to call him when I got back to the city, and maybe we could hang out sometime."

Ava and I both squealed. "You're going to, right?" I asked. "Call him?"

Bailey shrugged. "Maybe." Then she grinned, and her nose crinkled up the way it sometimes did when she was super-happy. "Definitely!"

Bailey's mom started the car, and Bailey blew us both kisses before they took off. "Mwah!"

Moments later, Ava was driving off with her sister and her dad too, and then it was just my family left. Coco and I piled into the backseat, and as my mom navigated the car down the winding dirt road—back toward civilization—I thought about how much had changed since the first time I'd been on that road.

"I think we got a lot of great ideas pulled together this month. We're going to have some good campaigns to share with our clients this fall." My dad was obviously very cheerful in the front seat. Then he turned to look at me. "You survived?"

I smiled at him. "Definitely. I had a great time."

He looked surprised. "What got into you? Who took my whining daughter?" he asked.

"No one. Nothing," I said, annoyed that I was getting criticized, even when I was trying to be optimistic. "I really did have a great time. Thanks for bringing me along."

My dad gave me a look that made it obvious he thought demons had possessed me, then quietly turned back to watch the road ahead.

I gazed up into the canopy of trees that had seemed so dark and ominous when we'd first arrived at the lake. Now, they reminded me of thunderstorms and swimming with friends and roasted marshmallows and Liar and Spy and Canoe Wars. Once I'd let myself just enjoy it, I had realized the woods was full of all good things, nothing creepy at all. Except raccoons, which still skeeved me out. Oh, and ticks. And mosquitoes. Also, sometimes the weeds at the bottom of the lake were a little spooky. Okay, so maybe there were a few creepy things—I was still a city girl at heart. But the good things were so much better than the bad that I learned how to overlook some of the *ew* stuff after a while.

Coco was already fast asleep beside me, so I closed my eyes and let my mind drift off, hoping I'd dream of summer.

I woke up to the sound of my cell phone ringing.

"Izzy!" My mom snapped at me from the front seat. "Can you answer that? That song is dreadful."

I dug around, looking for my phone. I guess my mom had tossed it back once we'd left the lake. I dug around on the floor, then searched the seats, cringing as my ringtone went on and on. Finally, I found it under Coco's butt. I wondered if my mom had put it there on purpose.

"Hello?" I said, realizing too late that Heidi's name was on the screen. She hated when her friends acted all formal on the phone—she was more of a "hey" sort of girl.

"*Hello?*" Heidi demanded from the other end. "What, you've been gone so long you deleted my number from your contacts or something? I get a 'hello,' not a 'hey' or a 'hi' or a 'I missed you like crazy, Heid!' You sound like your mom. *Hello? Hel-looo.*" As she teased me, she switched into a snooty old-lady voice that made her crack up.

"Hey, Heid. I did miss you."

"Are you back yet?" she blurted out. "We have to go shopping. Stat. School starts in four days. Four! And we have major outfit coordination to do."

I looked out the window and listened to her drone on. I sort of wasn't in the mood for Heidi, which was strange. For half the month, I'd been looking forward to getting back to see my friends, but now that we were almost back, I wasn't quite as psyched anymore. Somehow, I realized, I'd slept through almost the whole drive home—we were only a few miles from our house. That must have been why it was so hard for me to shake out of my sleepy stupor. "We're almost home," I said. "We should be at my house in ten minutes."

"I'll tell Sylvie to have her mom swing by and pick you up first, then. She's dropping us off at the mall."

I looked down at my stained shorts and ratty tank top. It was a shirt I'd borrowed from Bailey a week or so ago, then forgotten to give back. "I'm disgusting," I said. "I should take a shower first."

"We don't have time," Heidi said bossily. "You can come, or you can not come—but if you want to be part of our outfit planning, be ready in ten minutes. We waited for you all month, but we're not waiting any longer."

"Wow," I said, slowly slipping back into the old routine. "Bossy much?"

"Shut up," Heidi said. I could hear the smile in her voice. We always talked to each other like this. One of us would push, and the other person would bite back.

"No, you shut up," I said back. The snippiness didn't feel as natural, but I tried to play my part. I wished Heidi and I could just have a normal conversation where we were *kind* to each other, but it didn't really work that way with us—we both kind of liked being sarcastic and snappy. It was our thing. "I'll be ready when I'm ready. You know you're going to wait for me."

"Whatever," Heidi said. "Missed you, you know."

"I missed you, too," I said. "See you in a few."

I hung up and tucked my phone into my bag, back where it belonged. Once I put on normal clothes, I would feel complete again.

"You're going out?" My mom asked, glancing at me in the rearview mirror.

"Yep," I answered.

"Were you planning to ask if it's okay?"

"I think you owe me, after holding me hostage for the last month, don't you?" I stared back at her. Finally, in the nicest voice I could manage, I said, "Could I please, pretty please, see my friends tonight after you've kept me from talking to them for the last three weeks?"

My mom sighed. "Fine."

When we pulled into our driveway a few minutes later, Sylvie and her mom were already there waiting. Sylvie jumped out of the car and hugged me tightly. "You're finally back!" She backed up quickly. "Ew. You stink."

"Yeah," I said, shrugging. "I haven't showered in a while." I looked down at Bailey's tank top and cringed. It was an ugly tank top, but I'd been super-comfortable the last week or so (I'd worn it almost every day since I borrowed it from her).

I knew I probably looked awful, but honestly, I hadn't even looked in the mirror all day. Looks never seemed to matter at the resort. Suddenly, I realized we were back in civilization where stuff like that did make a difference again.

"You need to change," Sylvie said, pushing me toward our front door. "Immediately. Where did you get that ugly tank top?"

"I borrowed it from a friend at the resort." My parents were busy carrying stuff in, so I hustled over to the car and grabbed my bag. "It's comfy."

"No *friend* would ever let someone be seen in something like that," Sylvie said. "You're back in public. Fix yourself, and let's go."

I went inside and dropped my stuff on my floor. After I'd changed into a cute pair of shorts and a clean tank top, I quickly tossed all my dirty clothes in the hamper and put my suitcase away. Hopefully, my mom would notice the gesture. I pulled a brush through my hair and peeked in the mirror. Not cute. I pulled my hair back into a ponytail, dabbed on some lip gloss, swiped nail polish remover across my finger-tips, and headed back outside.

"Much better," Sylvie said, nodding.

As we drove to Heidi's house, Sylvie talked nonstop.

"Ohmigod, Heidi has been driving me crazy," she whispered, so her mom wouldn't hear. "She's been obsessing over Jake Theisen, and he's literally all she can talk about. Now that you're back, hopefully she'll just chill out about it, since I can't listen to her, and blah, blah, blah . . ."

I let Sylvie ramble on and on, but since I had nothing to contribute, I didn't really say much. She complained about Heidi until we got to Heidi's house. Once Heidi was in the car, they talked over each other trying to tell me about all the stupid things Cianna Jackson and Emily Kim had done at Sylvie's birthday party. Then they told me about the weekend at Heidi's dad's lake place. As they talked about how they'd spent most of the weekend inside the cabin, I found myself realizing I hadn't really missed much at all. I was sure I'd had a lot more fun at the resort with Bailey and Ava.

"So how was your month of torture?" Heidi asked finally, after we'd been walking through the mall for fifteen minutes already.

"It was pretty good, actually."

"Did you put those losers in their place?" Heidi asked.

It was obvious she was talking about Bailey and Ava, since I'd told my friends who was there with me. But I pretended I didn't know what she was talking about. "Who?"

"Bailey Something and Ava Whatever," Sylvie said, pulling us into one of our favorite stores. "Did they follow you around all summer?"

Before I had to answer, two other girls from our class came into the store and Heidi and Sylvie forgot all about their question. For the next two hours, I did my best to act as normal as possible, but I was seriously distracted by the thoughts that were swirling around in my head. I was freaked out about what was going to happen when we got back to school, when Bailey and Ava were around us every day. And I was dreading what might happen when I told my friends about how much fun I'd had during my month at the lake.

I'd only been home for a few hours, but I could already tell it was going to be harder to go back to normal than I'd ever imagined it could be. I'd been gone for just one month, but in that time so much had changed. And now I wasn't even sure the old "normal" was something I wanted anymore.

Chapter Fifteen

~~~~~~~~~~

When school started a few days later, Heidi and I got a ride from Sylvie's mom—just like always. Sylvie and I were both zoned for the bus, but only losers rode the bus, so we always got her mom to drive us.

My friends and I were perfectly coordinated, down to our boots, even. We'd all gotten these adorable black boots at the mall a few days before. Along with the boots, I was wearing a black skirt, baby-blue ruffled shirt, and blue-and-black-plaid tights. Sylvie had chosen the same skirt, a pink shirt, and pink-and-black-plaid tights. Heidi stepped out of the car in a matching purple-and-black ensemble. We looked perfect.

As we hopped out of the car, I surveyed the scene. I saw a few groups of kids from our class, who were all watching us. Sylvie leaned over to whisper, "They all *so* wish they were us right now."

Heidi giggled. "How cute do we look? *So* cute."

I just nodded and smiled. Across the front lawn, a few of the buses were unloading. Even at a distance, Bailey's copper hair made it easy to spot her emerging from one. I watched as she greeted Ava, who had come out of a different bus, and they met up with a few of their other friends.

"Distracted much?" Heidi asked, then wrapped her arm through mine and pulled me toward school. My friends were on either side of me, and I took the center spot. I was always in the middle. Maybe it's because I'm the tallest, maybe not, but for some reason we always walked in a line that went Heidi, Izzy, Sylvie. As we strutted toward the front doors, people stepped away, clearing a path for us.

On either side of me, my friends smiled and flipped their hair. "Oh my God, look at her outfit," Heidi giggled, pointing at Safia Neri from our class.

"Do you think someone dared her to cut her hair like that? It hurts my eyes to look at it," Sylvie sneered, as we passed Makayla Unger. Makayla waved timidly at us as we went by, and Sylvie smiled and waved back to her. "Hi-iiii! Cute haircut."

We found my locker first, then Heidi's, then Sylvie's. Everything we did was just the same as we did it last year. There was a routine we followed, and it was comforting to know it would be the same this year. But something felt off. I couldn't get into the conversation, and I felt like part of me wasn't ready to be back at school.

"Why so quiet, Izzy?" Sylvie said, as she and I leaned against Heidi's locker, waiting for her to unpack her bag. I knew we'd be waiting a while—Heidi always brought a million things to decorate her locker with, and this year was no exception. She put a mirror up, then several pictures of the three of us, and a poster of some runner she's obsessed with (Heidi's super into running, especially short distances where she doesn't sweat a lot and ruin her makeup).

"You are not at all yourself," Heidi added. Someone bumped into her from behind, and Heidi turned around to give whoever it was a look of death. The guy—Brandon, Brendan, Ben?—backed away, scared.

"I'm not quiet," I said.

"You haven't even made one comment about Sara Anne Brown's outfit, and I *know* you must have something to say." Heidi gestured across the hall toward the locker of one of our elementary school friends.

Sara Anne Brown and I had been pretty good friends until third grade, and then she got lice. At the time, I told everyone that it wasn't a surprise she had lice, since Sara Anne's house was always nasty (not true). I'd maybe pushed the story a little too far when I added that I thought they probably had bedbugs, too. Part of the reason I told the story is that I still think *I* was the one who gave Sara Anne lice in the first place. I never told anyone I'd had it at all. . . . It was less embarrassing if people thought Sara Anne was the source of it all.

Today, Sara Anne was wearing a pair of navy-blue pants—slacks, really—that she must have stolen out of her mother's closet. They were too big and a really awful color, and she'd paired them with this shirt that seriously had a pony on it.

I closed my eyes, wishing I could erase what I'd seen. It was almost impossible not to say something about an outfit that was *that* horrible, but I found I sort of didn't want to say anything at all. Last year, I would have made fun of her— loudly. But that day, all I could think about was the time Sara Anne had let me stay over three nights in a row when my dad was out of town, just so I wouldn't have to spend all that time home alone with my mom.

"It's not that bad," I said finally. Both Heidi's and Sylvie's mouths hung open.

"You're kidding, right?" Sylvie blurted out. She raised her voice until she was practically screaming, then blurted out, "Isabella Caravelli cannot *stand* navy pants. Or slacks. Or trousers. They should be illegal. Right, Izzy?"

I cringed, and looked across the hall at Sara Anne. She had obviously heard Sylvie, since she glanced at me for the briefest second, slammed her locker closed, and skulked away.

"Why did you do that?" I demanded. "That was so mean."

Sylvie giggled. "It was for her own good. She needs to learn that navy-blue mom pants aren't doing her any favors. She looks like a lunch lady or something," she said. "Heidi, can you get your butt moving? I want to do a quick walk past Henry Ehler's locker. He spent the whole summer on his parents' boat, and he looks delish."

"First we're going by Jake's locker, though," Heidi said, pouting her lips to reapply her lip gloss. "You promised."

"I did not," Sylvie snapped. "Besides, I think you probably need to talk to Izzy about Jake."

"What?" I said, confused. On our way to the mall the other day, Sylvie had been telling me all about how Heidi was interested in Jake Theisen. I remembered because she'd been complaining about how obsessed Heidi had been all summer. I'd listened to her whining about it long enough that I couldn't possibly forget. "What do *I* have to do with Heidi and Jake?"

"Remember?" Sylvie said, turning to wink at me so Heidi couldn't see. "You told me *you're* super-interested in Jake too. Didn't you tell me you're thinking of asking him to the fall dance?"

I stared at her. "No," I said, seriously confused.

"Yes, you did," Sylvie insisted. "Remember how you told me that you and Jake had that 'moment' at Sophia's party right before you left for your dad's horrible work trip this summer? On our way to the mall the other day, you *just* told me you were going to make sure he was into you this year. Remember?" She winked again.

"I'm not interested in Jake Theisen," I said, pulling my eyebrows together. Then realization hit—Sylvie was just trying to get me to go after him because Heidi wanted him too. This was exactly the kind of game we usually played with each other, but I didn't want any part in it. "Heidi's interested in Jake, so I'm not going to get in her way. It's, like, a friend code or something to stay away from your friend's crush."

I looked over at Heidi and saw she was close to tears. "Really?" she asked, her eyes big and hopeful.

"Really," I said, nodding. "Friends don't go after friends' guys. It's not cool."

"Oh," Sylvie said with a huff. "I didn't realize the rules had changed." She looked annoyed and sounded super-sarcastic when she said, "And obviously, what Izzy says, goes."

"I like Izzy's rule, even if she *is* acting weird today." Heidi said, slamming her locker closed.

When I turned to head toward Sylvie's locker, I spotted Bailey and Ava walking down the hall toward us. I watched as they got closer. My friends already thought I was acting like a nutjob, so how freaked out were they going to be when I actually said hi to Bailey and Ava? I still hadn't told Heidi or Sylvie about how close I'd gotten to my two summer friends, so it was going to come as a total surprise.

Bailey and Ava were laughing about something, and they didn't notice me at first. But when they were just a few feet away, Bailey looked up and saw me. Just as our eyes locked, Heidi poked me in the side and said, "Ready? Let's move."

I looked away from Bailey for just a second, but when I looked back, she'd turned away again. Ava glanced at me for the briefest of seconds, but neither of us said anything.

"Hi, guys," I said, my voice catching. I'm not sure my words carried over the sounds in the hall. Neither of them said anything back.

"Did they just ignore you?" Sylvie asked, staring at the backs of Bailey's and Ava's heads. "Hel-*lo*? Did you just *ignore* Isabella Caravelli? That is so not cool."

Bailey and Ava kept on walking, without looking back. I don't know why they were ignoring me, but it hurt.

"It's fine, Sylvie," I said. "Just forget it."

"That's not at all fine. When you say hi to people, they're supposed to say hi back. It's called manners."

"They didn't hear me," I said, trying to steer their focus away from Bailey and Ava. "I'll catch up with them later."

Heidi gawked at me. "Excuse me? You'll catch up with them later?"

"Yeah. They're the two girls I spent August with at the resort."

"Um, yes," Sylvie said in a totally condescending voice. "We know that. We get that you spent a month with them, but it's not like that means you have to suddenly be BFFs with two nobodies now that you're back in civilization with us."

"They're my friends now," I said, starting to get angry. "I

really like them, and I think if you gave them a chance, you'd probably like them too."

Heidi laughed. "Yes, I'm sure we'd all have just the bestest time dressing up our dollies and trying on Mommy's makeup."

I stared her down, trying to make her stop. It was my Isabella Caravelli look, the one that seemed to scare and intimidate so many people, but it didn't have the effect I wanted on one of my best friends.

"Seriously, Iz," Heidi said, still laughing. "That Ava girl looks like she's about nine, and she never says anything. She's like a little mouse with a really unfortunate haircut. Do you think she gave a monkey at the zoo a pair of scissors and asked it to please, pretty please cut her bangs for her?" She giggled, amusing herself. "I know you only hung out with the two of them this summer because they did everything you told them to do. They were like your minions, right? It was a classic Izzy pity party."

As Heidi spit out the last of her awful words, I noticed that Sylvie was smiling just a tiny bit and carefully watching something over my shoulder. I turned to look, and saw that Ava and Bailey were suddenly standing right behind me.

"Excuse me," Bailey said, refusing to make eye contact

again. She pointed. "I think this is my locker. Can I get by?"

I stepped to the side, and watched as Bailey fiddled with the combination on her lock. Ava stood beside her. While Bailey unloaded her bag and grabbed a notebook for first period, neither she nor Ava said anything.

I had no idea how much of Heidi's rant they had heard, and I had no idea what I could say to make it clear that I *hadn't* been talking about them. My best friends—at least, the girls I'd *thought* were my best friends—were being absolutely horrible. And I was stuck in the middle of it.

I hoped all it would take was a conversation with Bailey and Ava to sort things out. But sometimes, I knew, words meant nothing. Especially when you were fighting against your own reputation—and my reputation was Mean Girl. I had a feeling it wasn't going to be easy to prove that I had changed, or to convince anyone that Heidi and Sylvie's words were *their* words and not mine.

But I knew I had to try.

Chapter Sixteen

~~~~~~~~~~~~~~~~~~~

It turned out Bailey and I had third-period history together, but I couldn't get her alone to talk. I tried to sit in an open seat right behind her, but Brenna Thomson flagged me down, and by the time I was able to squirm away from her annoying gossip about something totally inconsequential, all the seats near Bailey were taken.

At lunch, I sat at a table with Sylvie and Heidi, as usual. This year, we got to move one table closer to the windows—to the rectangular table that was right next to some of the soccer guys, including Henry and Jake. Only one table was better than ours, but that was the one the eighth-grade posse (which was ruled by Skylar, the captain of the dance team) sat at. Next year, their big round table right by the windows would be ours.

The lunchroom operated on an informal reservation system, and it had always worked that way. Everyone knew who went where, and anyone who tried to break the lunchroom rules would pay. As I munched on my bagel that day, I wondered why it mattered so much—and why we stressed out about who would fill the other five seats at our table. It took so much time and energy to control the lunchroom-table situation that, by the time we figured out who would sit where, we hardly had any time to talk at all.

Bailey and Ava must have decided to eat outside or something, since I didn't see either of them in the cafeteria—or again for the rest of the day. As soon as school was over, my friends met me at my locker practically before the bell had finished ringing.

"Hang out at my house?" Sylvie suggested. My locker wasn't even closed yet.

"Definitely," Heidi sighed. "I need to go through my routine a few more times before dance team auditions tomorrow." She flipped her hair over one shoulder, and I realized for the first time just how often she did that. After another flip to the other side, she pulled out her lip gloss and leaned against the locker next to mine. Maren Fuller, who belonged to that locker, walked up seconds later and just stood there, trying to figure out if it was a good idea to ask Heidi to move or not. Heidi ignored her, and finally Maren walked away. "Not that I'm worried about auditions, obvs."

I rolled my eyes. I *knew* Heidi was nervous about dance tryouts, but she always tried to make it seem like she was a shoo-in for the team. "You're not at all nervous?" I asked, trying to get her to fess up. I wanted us to be more honest with each other, wanted us to be the kind of best friends who tell each other things and don't backstab. The kind of friends who can confess things to each other, and not worry about being judged.

"Not really," Heidi said confidently. "Tryouts are just a formality. I can't think of who *would* get in, other than Sylvie and me."

I thought about Ava, and how hard she'd been working on her routine all summer. There were only ten slots on the team, and six of those would be filled with girls who were returning to the team from last year. That meant there were only four open spots on the team. I knew Ava was a much better dancer than Heidi, but I also knew Ava was sort of a nobody, and the captains of the team—the eighth graders who controlled the top lunchroom table—were obsessed with making sure the team had the "right kind" of people.

Skill was only one little part of who got a slot on the team, which I'd begun to realize was really stupid.

"I just don't want you to get your hopes up and then be disappointed," I said. "I'm sure there are a ton of amazing people trying out, so don't go in expecting it to be a sure thing."

Heidi sniffed. "You are a major bummer today, Izzy," she said. "And that's a really nasty thing to say to your best friend. Aren't you supposed to have my back?"

"Yeah," I said. "I'm sorry. I'm sure you'll be amazing." I slammed my locker closed and slung my bag over my shoulder. "I guess I'm just sort of freaking out about school starting or something. It feels different this year."

I was about to add something about Bailey and Ava, to tell Heidi and Sylvie how mean and hurtful their words had been that morning. But before I could figure out how to word it so it wouldn't sound like I was scolding them, I spotted Bailey at the end of the hall. She was walking into the disgusting bathroom right at the end of the band hallway. Ava was with her. I realized I had to seize the opportunity. "Guys, actually, I kind of feel sick. Maybe I'm getting the flu or something. I need to run to the bathroom for a sec—" I trailed off as I hustled down the hall. I went quickly, hoping they wouldn't follow me.

"Iz?" Sylvie called after me.

After a beat, I heard Heidi say, "Should we offer to hold her hair while she pukes or something?"

I guess they decided the answer was no, since neither of them followed me. I stepped into the bathroom, and found Bailey and Ava at the sinks washing their hands. "Hey," I said, breathless. I guess maybe I'd been a little too into my about-to-puke routine, since now I was totally winded. I probably didn't need to hustle quite as much as I had.

"Hi, Izzy," Bailey said, looking over my shoulder to see who was with me. She visibly relaxed when she saw I was alone.

"How was your first day?" I asked.

"Fine," Ava said quietly. I noticed she was wearing my headband. She caught me looking at it and said, "Oh my gosh. I'm so sorry. I forgot to give this back." She pulled it off her head and thrust it toward me. Her hair was sticking up all over the place. "Do you want it back? I don't have lice or anything." She was talking so quietly it was almost a whisper. It was like she was just a shadow of the person she'd become around me when we were at the lake.

"If you had lice, don't you think I probably would have caught it by now?" I asked, trying for a light and airy tone. "We spent the last few weeks sharing clothes and pillows, so I'm obviously not worried about it." I paused, then added,

"Anyway, I don't want it back. It looks better on you."

"Okay," said Ava, and returned it to her hair. "Thanks."

"You guys, this morning . . . ," I started, unsure of exactly how much they'd heard Heidi and Sylvie say before school. "I don't know if you heard what my friends were saying this morning, but I just wanted you to know that I had a great time with you this summer, and I don't want you to think I, like, only hung out with you out of pity or something." I realized that sounded terrible the second I said it, but I wasn't sure how to rephrase it now. "I mean—"

Bailey cut me off. "Look, Izzy, we just assumed you'd act like we didn't even exist once we got back to school. We're trying to move on too. So it's not really a big deal."

"And honestly—" Ava said. She broke off, swallowed, then said, "We'd kind of prefer if we weren't even on your radar at all. If you could just *not* talk about us when you're with Heidi and Sylvie, that would probably be best. We don't really need to be the subject of your mean-girl pranks this year."

"I wouldn't!" I said, my eyes stinging from tears that came out of nowhere. I couldn't believe that after the month we'd spent together, they would ever think that I'd do anything to intentionally hurt them. But even though I believed I had changed, I knew that the Isabella Caravelli everyone knew at this school totally *would* pull mean-girl pranks on someone who was supposedly a friend.

But I was sick of mean-girl pranks—they were, well, *mean*. And the fact is, I was a lot happier at the lake when I was spending time just having fun with Ava and Bailey than I *ever* was when Heidi and Sylvie and I were putting people down. I liked the person I'd become when I was out of school and away from my own reputation, and I sort of wanted a piece of that *other* me to stick around. I liked the Izzy that Bailey and Ava knew, and I wasn't so sure I liked the Isabella Caravelli everyone else at Southwest was used to. That girl was sort of a snob.

"You guys," I said, sounding desperate, "I really want to find a way for us to be friends at school, too. Maybe we could hang out after school one day, or you guys could come over? Heidi and Sylvie are nice once you get to know them. What if we ate lunch together tomorrow, in a big group? You can sit at our table."

Ava smiled sadly. "I don't think so," she whispered. "I loved hanging out with you this summer, but I find it hard to believe that you're going to change for *good*. People just don't change into a new person in one summer."

Bailey nodded along. "We've got to go, or we'll miss the bus," she said, backing toward the bathroom door. They both waved to me as they hustled off. "See ya, Izzy," Bailey called over her shoulder.

I stood in the bathroom for a while, trying to think. I had no idea what I was supposed to do. I'd apologized, and I was trying to be nicer—but I wondered if what Ava had said was true. *Could* a person change? Could *I*? Maybe not. Maybe we all have a part to play in middle school, and I was just messing up everything by trying to be someone I wasn't.

After a few minutes had passed—and the stench of the automatic air freshener started to make me sick—I slipped back out into the hall to return to my friends. When I got back to my locker, they both sort of backed away from me. "No offense, Iz," Heidi said slowly, "but I really don't want to get sick before dance team auditions, so maybe we shouldn't hang out this afternoon?"

"Yeah," I agreed, kind of relieved to have an excuse not to hang out with my best friends. I needed some time to think, and an all-afternoon gossip fest wasn't going to let me do that. "Maybe that's a good idea."

"We'll pick you up in the morning, okay?" Sylvie said. "Don't forget—tomorrow's outfit is jeans and the T-shirts we got at the mall last week, okay?"

"I won't forget," I said, waving weakly as my friends hurried away from me as fast as possible. I sighed, and finished gathering stuff into my bag. It wasn't until I slammed my locker closed and headed for the side door that I realized Heidi was my ride home. I'd missed the buses (not that I'd take one anyway), and my friends were probably long gone by now. I was stranded.

I couldn't believe they'd just abandoned me. It was like they'd totally forgotten that we were all riding together or something! Frustrated, I sunk down on a bench by the front doors and pulled out my phone. I could call my mom, but I knew she'd be really annoyed if she had to come all the way to school to get me. She was under deadline for her freelance projects, and anyway, she never drove me to or from school. It was as if she didn't realize the bus was social suicide. I *could* walk, but it was really far, and my new black boots were already rubbing wrong. Then I had an idea.

I dialed, hoping my dad would pick up. He did!

"Hi, Dad," I said, trying not to let my bummer of a day sneak into my voice. He could always sense stuff like that, even when I thought I was doing a good job covering it up. "What are you doing?"

"Working," he said. He sounded distracted. "What do you need, Isabella?"

"Um . . . ," I said, realizing it was stupid to have called him. I hadn't called my dad in the middle of the workday in more than a year—probably not since fifth grade, even, when we started drifting apart. After a few seconds slipped by, I realized I'd said "um," which was one of my dad's pet-peeve words. Maybe he wouldn't notice my communication error. "I was just wondering if, maybe, you—uh—wanted to leave work a little early and maybe go biking or something?"

For some reason, a bike ride with my dad was the one thing I wanted to do. I knew if I went home and sat alone, I'd just end up calling Heidi. It was habit, and I had to start breaking some habits if I was going to try to change for good. Also, my dad always used to have really good advice when I was stuck on something. I needed some advice. "Maybe we could stop and get some ice cream to celebrate the first day of school?"

There was a long pause, then my dad sighed. "Izzy—" he said, his voice a warning.

"Never mind," I said quickly. I couldn't handle being rejected a second time in the same day—first Bailey and Ava, then my dad. I was trying to be nice! Why wasn't anyone responding? And why on earth did I call my dad, when I knew he didn't have time for me? "It was just an idea."

There was silence. Then my dad said, "Actually, I like that idea. We haven't done something to commemorate your first day of school in a while. Ice cream sounds good. I like the way you're thinking."

Fifteen minutes later, Dad pulled up in front of Southwest. I hopped into the front seat and smiled at him. He smiled back. "Backseat, kid."

"Dad," I pleaded. "I'm almost thirteen."

He looked at me for a long moment as though he was just realizing I wasn't a little kid anymore. "That you are. Sometimes it's hard to believe you're so old." He looked like he was going to give in and let me sit up front with him like a normal person, but then he jabbed his thumb toward the backseat. "Still, it's my job to keep you safe until you're off to college. So backseat it is."

I scowled. "Car seat regulations allow a twelve-year-old in front. Especially a *tall* twelve-year-old."

Dad lifted his eyebrows at me. "Hey, I'm happy to leave you here if you don't like my rules. But you're the one who needs a ride and called your dad."

He had a point. "Thanks for picking me up," I said when I'd gotten myself buckled in to the backseat. I'd briefly debated asking him to help me buckle my seat belt—just as a joke—but figured he wouldn't think it was that funny. He'd probably assume I was trying to be "smart."

"My pleasure," he said. "Don't you usually get a ride home with Heidi or Sylvie?"

"Yeah," I said. "But it was a long day, and I kind of needed some time away."

"Aha!" Dad glanced at me in his rearview mirror. There was a hint of a smile on his lips. "So your biking request was all just a ruse to get me to pick you up? Or did you actually want to spend time with your old man?"

"Ew! Did you really just call yourself 'old man'? And yes, I really do want to go biking. I mean, I just need some time away from my friends—not *alone* alone time." I decided it couldn't hurt to tell him I'd been missing him too. "Anyway, I realized we haven't really spent much quality time together over the last couple years, and I just thought it might be fun to hang out."

"Thanks for suggesting it," he said. After a long pause, he said, "I'm sorry we don't spend as much time together as we used to."

"It's okay," I said.

Then Dad had to go and get all cheesy on me. He pulled the car to the side of the road so he could turn around in his seat and look right at me to say, "I've missed our father-daughter dates. A lot. As much as you hated your mother and me for dragging you along to the lake this summer, I think some quality time away did something good for all of us. I mean, when's the last time you picked hanging out with your old man over hanging out with your friends?"

"Okay, old man," I said, grinning. He was right, but I wasn't going to admit it. "Enough with the emo fest. Let's just hang out without making a big deal out of it, okay?"

Dad laughed. "Okay, okay. But just so you know, I like seeing my cheerful Izzy again. You have such a pretty smile."

A million smart retorts flew into my mouth, but I held them all in. Because, honestly, it felt good to hear my dad say something really nice about me, instead of something critical. For once, I felt like I'd done something right—just by smiling and making an effort to be nice to my dad. "Thanks," I said finally, my smile widening. "Now can we move along, mister? People are starting to stare."

Chapter Seventeen

Dad and I ended up having an awesome afternoon. Instead of biking, we walked around the lake near our house—it was Dad's idea, so that Coco could come along. We made a stop for ice cream at the little shop near the beach on the far side of the lake. It was the place we used to go to when I was little, where they serve up huge double-scoop cones, with a tiny third scoop right on top—so you get an itty-bitty sample of an extra flavor, just for fun. They even had these little ice-cream-cone-shaped biscuits for dogs, so Coco was super-happy too.

The ice cream tasted good, like summer. While we walked and talked—with a few stops to let Coco take a dip in the lake—I filled Dad in on the weirdness with Bailey and Ava.

He actually had some things for me to try! Most of his suggestions were about watching my tone of voice and adjusting my body language and being vigilant about using carefully chosen words (cue TV commercial background music), but he also had a few other ideas that I was willing to try. By the time we'd finished a second lap around the lake, I had a fully formed plan in my head. Whether it would work or not was another matter. . . .

When we got home, Dad suggested I find Mom and ask her to help me with my big idea. After I told her what I had planned, she seemed really excited that I was coming to her for help. I think it surprised both of us that we actually had a ton of fun getting me ready for the next day at school. By the end of the night, all three of us were laughing so hard I almost forgot how annoying my parents could be most of the time.

The next morning, as I got ready for school, I put on some music and danced around my room. My mom had washed Bailey's tank top, the one I'd borrowed at the lake, so I put it on with a cute skirt and a pair of sneakers. Coco watched me suspiciously, her head tucked between her two front paws on my bed.

"Today's going to be a good day, babe," I said, leaning down to kiss her wrinkly head. "I might die of embarrassment, but I think it's going to be worth it." Coco whimpered and put one paw on top of her nose, like she was hiding from something. "It *will* be worth it, right?" My puppy didn't answer, which was probably a good thing. I was sort of worried I was going a little bit crazy. If I suddenly started hearing my dog talk back, it was definitely a bad sign that I was totally nuts.

While I ate breakfast, Mom sat down at the table with me and talked . . . just talked. She didn't criticize, or pick on me, or even get on my case for eating sugar cereal. "Good luck today," she said as I put my bowl in the dishwasher. I looked at her, and she smiled. "You're going to be great, Izzy. "

When Heidi's mom picked me up for school, I ran outside before she honked and jumped into the car. I pulled my huge gym bag in after me and stuffed it down by my feet.

"What are you wearing?" Sylvie blurted out, poking her head between the headrests in the second row of Heidi's mom's SUV. "Those aren't jeans."

"Yeah," I said, shrugging. "I decided not to wear jeans today."

"We *agreed* to wear jeans," Sylvie said, obviously annoyed. "Heidi and I totally match, and you totally don't."

"Maybe we don't always need to match," I said, trying to

use my carefully chosen words and my carefully practiced tone of voice. "Maybe it sometimes looks a little snobby when we all have a version of the same thing on."

I heard Heidi's mom snicker in the front seat.

"Or maybe you just think you're better than us," Sylvie snapped.

"Not at all!" I protested, realizing my plan to not be all matchy-matchy with Sylvie and Heidi was kind of backfiring. I hadn't thought about the fact that they might be upset with me for backing out of our coordinated-outfit plan. That they might think I was acting superior.

"You could have at least told us," Heidi scoffed. She stared out the window, facing away from me.

I poked her in the arm, forcing her to look at me. "Yeah," I said, when she finally turned my way. "I should have told you I changed my plan. I didn't think you guys would be that upset. It's just jeans and a T-shirt," I muttered.

"Or a tank top and a skirt, if you're you," Sylvie grumbled. "Now Heidi and I just look like we're trying to be twins or something. It's not exactly the same effect if all *three* of us aren't wearing the same thing."

I rolled my eyes. "No one will even notice," I said, lowering my voice so Heidi's mom would stop listening in. I could see her craning her neck, trying to hear what we were talking about. "I just think that this year, we don't need to make such a big show of always doing everything the same. Sometimes I think it looks like we're deliberately excluding people, just to be rude."

"We *are* deliberately excluding people," Sylvie said. "And making it clear that *we* are best friends. Unless you're too good for us now?" She looked at me like she was challenging me to agree. "Unless you found someone better than us to be best friends with?"

"It's not that at all!" I said. I was relieved that we were pulling up in front of school, and we had to get out of the car quickly, before the school monitor gave Heidi's mom a warning for lingering too long.

"Look," I said, when we got out of the car. "We don't need matching outfits to prove that we're best friends, okay? I think sometimes it's probably just a little intimidating. I'm not saying we suddenly need to start sitting with the chess club at lunch, but maybe we don't always have to go out of our way to make other people feel like they're less amazing than us. Okay?"

Sylvie stared at me, openmouthed. "Did you get possessed over the summer or something? Oh my God, that Ava girl is probably a witch. I knew there was something weird about her."

I sighed. Okay, so my first attempt at modifying my reputation wasn't going well *at all*. Now my friends were getting even worse ideas about Ava and Bailey. And they also thought I was acting *really* crazy, and apparently also believed I think I'm too good for them. This was a disaster.

As we walked into school, Sylvie and Heidi both sulked beside me, looking sort of depressed in their matching jeans-and-T-shirt combos. "Guys, I didn't do this to hurt your feelings," I said, looking at both of them. Sylvie rolled her eyes. "Seriously. I should have thought to tell you I changed my mind about the matching outfits."

"Whatever," Heidi muttered.

I shook my head, annoyed that they were so annoyed that I'd messed up their outfits. *I* was the one who looked like I didn't fit in . . . not them. I didn't understand why it was such a big deal. "So are you ready for tryouts this afternoon?" I asked, while they waited for me to unload my stuff at my locker.

"Definitely," Heidi said, perking up a little. "Are you coming to watch? You'll cheer for me?"

"Of course," I said, shoving my gym bag to the bottom of

my locker. I couldn't look at her or Sylvie, since I was keeping a little something from them. Just one teensy detail that I was sure would surprise them later. But not in a bad way—I hoped it would be a good way! Though after the outfit mess, maybe they didn't like my surprises.

I briefly considered telling them about my plan for that afternoon, but I knew they'd try to talk me out of it. And I didn't want anyone to talk me out of it, since it was Part Two of Operation: Reputation Makeover. "I'll definitely be there."

The day seemed to drag by, but finally the last bell rang and the time had come for dance team tryouts. As I walked through the hall to my locker after seventh period, it felt like the whole school was buzzing about tryouts.

I knew there would be a ton of people there—both watching *and* dancing—which is why a part of me really wanted to back out of my plan (no one would ever know that I'd chickened out . . . except me and my parents). But I wanted to prove that I could be a good friend, so I was going to go and do what I'd decided to do after talking to my dad the day before.

I was ready to sit in the bleachers that lined the gym and cheer for all my friends.

And I was also ready to dance in front of everyone, even though I knew I'd look like a fool.

On our walk yesterday, Dad had told me that relatability was the biggest key to changing my reputation. Apparently, this was a big public relations and media thing that he sometimes used with their agency clients. Sometimes, he'd told me, when companies started to get a bad reputation, they'd adjust their advertising so it focused on things that would make them more likeable and relatable to the general public.

For instance, in print advertising, a certain company would focus their message on their over-the-top charity donation programs that helped people. Or in their TV commercials, they'd make a point of featuring "regular Joes" who worked in one of the company's stores or in their production plant. The point of this was, I guess, to get the rest of the world to believe a horrible company was less like a giant money-sucking retailer or manufacturer, and more of a place that employed nice, normal people from the local community. The way my dad described it made the whole thing seem kind of sneaky, but I guess it worked. I think my dad is really good at what he does.

The way this whole thing came up was, I'd told Dad that sometimes—maybe—people at our school thought my friends and I could be a little exclusive and snobbish. I even admitted that some people thought I could be a little bit mean (this didn't seem to totally surprise him). I told him I was hoping to figure out some way to get some of the other kids in our grade—most important, Ava and Bailey—to believe that I'd changed and that I was not actually a horrible person. Mostly, I wanted people to know that I didn't think I was better than them and that I wasn't always looking for ways to embarrass and humiliate other people.

Somehow, my dad had managed to convince me that if I could push my pride to the side and audition for dance team, then I would look like I was somehow more relatable to everyone else. "Let people see your flaws," he'd said. Dad knew I was a terrible dancer—I'd inherited one left foot from my mom, the other from my dad.

When I thought about opening up and letting people see my flaws, it made me want to puke. I didn't want anyone to know I had *any* flaws, but I knew my dad maybe had a point. So my plan was to go and cheer for my friends—*all* of my friends—as loudly as I could, and then get up there and risk major embarrassment by dancing in front of half the school. How relatable was *that*? Very.

I hastily grabbed my gym bag out of my locker and met

up with Sylvie and Heidi in the hall outside the gym. They were so obsessed with the fact that tryouts were about to start that they didn't even notice that I was following them into the locker rooms.

"Do you think Skylar Hendricks still likes Madonna?" Heidi asked Sylvie as they carved out a corner of the locker room for themselves. Heidi had decided to dance to "Like a Prayer," a Madonna song that she'd only picked because she'd heard the captain of the squad loved it. It was a smart strategy, but a really hard song to dance to, so Heidi was sort of out of her league. "I know she was obsessed with her last year, but what if she hates Madonna this year?"

"I guess you'll find out," Sylvie shrugged. She slipped into her short-shorts and tank top, then looked over at me. "Why are you changing?"

It wasn't a question so much as an accusation. She blatantly stared as I slipped on shorts under my skirt. "I decided to try out," I said casually, hoping they wouldn't laugh. "I figured I might as well give it a shot."

"I thought dance team conflicted with soccer?" Heidi said, narrowing her eyes. "Is this just another way for you to humiliate us? You're going to go out there and dance like a total rock star and make the rest of us look like idiots?"

"No, believe me," I said quietly, leaning in closer to them. The locker room was filling up with other people who were changing for tryouts, and I didn't want everyone to hear me. "You guys, the thing is . . . I'm a terrible dancer. I just learned how to dance with even a little bit of rhythm this summer." I shrugged and slipped my T-shirt on over my sports bra. "But I do think it would be really amazing if we were all on the team together, and just because I'm totally freaked out about embarrassing myself—well, that's kind of a dumb reason to not even try. So I'm just going to go out there and see what happens. I want to be here to support you and be a part of this, even if it means I'm going to end up looking like a moron."

I smiled, thinking about how impressed my mom had been the night before when I'd told her what I was planning to do. Of course, at first, she looked shocked. Then she told me she'd always wished she had the nerve to try out for her high school's dance team. While I practiced my routine, she ended up having a ton of good ideas about how to make it better. I was still going to look like a mess, but at least I'd managed to piece together a routine in less than one day that was somewhat decent.

Sylvie glared at me. "You're a bad dancer? Since when?"

I nodded. "The worst. Since forever. Haven't you noticed that I *never* dance?" Last year, at our first middle school dance, I'd somehow convinced all my friends that dancing in a group in front of everyone—as a sixth grader—was the surest way of looking desperate for all of middle school (the rules didn't apply to slow dancing with a guy, obviously). They believed me, so I was spared the public humiliation all year long. A group of us just stood along the wall during the fast songs and made fun of other girls who looked like they were having a lot more fun than we were.

"But you're going to try out anyway?" Heidi asked, smiling a tiny bit. "Why? It's like self-inflicted torture. How embarrassing."

She was totally right. I was setting myself up for major embarrassment. There were probably other ways to convince people that I wasn't a self-centered brat. But Ava and Bailey would be watching dance tryouts, and hopefully they'd understand what I was trying to do. They knew how much I worried about humiliating myself.

I hung my clothes inside a locker, and slammed it closed. "Here's the thing," I said, as we walked out toward the gym. "I'll look so bad that it's going to make the rest of you look amazing in comparison."

Sylvie rolled her eyes. "You are seriously messed. I really hope there's some other reason you're doing this that you're just not telling us about."

Heidi linked her arm through mine and added, "I personally can't *wait* to see what your master plan is, since you *must* have something else up your sleeve. There's no way Isabella Caravelli would intentionally embarrass herself without a reason." She laughed. "I seriously hope whatever you're planning is worth the humiliation."

"It will be," I said. I knew my friends thought I had some big prank planned. There was no reason for me to tell them the real deal—that this was just one part of my master plan to change my reputation. I knew it would be worth it.

At least, I *hoped* it would be.

Chapter Eighteen

zzy!" A few people waved to me as we made our way into the gym—people I knew I'd been mean to at various times, but who always seemed to forgive me. I smiled and waved back, but my stomach felt like it was being squeezed inside someone's fist.

Heidi and Sylvie stood tall beside me. I was grateful they were there, holding me up in a way. If my friends had walked away, I was sure I would have fallen over because I was so nervous. I glanced around at the faces that surrounded me and noticed that some girls from our grade were whispering and pointing my way. The sixth graders all just looked completely terrified. I could relate. I held my chin up and tried to look calm, but I was seriously scared I was going to trip over my own feet.

We all went over to the sign-up sheet that was hanging by the main gym door and printed our names on the list. We were toward the top—most people hadn't signed in yet. I guess that was good, since then I could get my turn over with early and just enjoy the rest of the tryouts. Maybe by the time everyone else had gone, people would forget I'd ever made a fool of myself at all.

Ha! I thought, my heart pounding. *As if.*

"Isabella!" Skylar Hendricks waved me over to a long table where she was standing with some of the other girls who were returning to the team from last year. Skylar and I were sort of friends, I guess. Not that we ever hung out outside school, but we were nice enough to each other in the hallway. I'd never tried to date any of her ex-boyfriends—there were a *lot* of them, but they were all sort of jerks—and I think that was enough to keep me off her Naughty List. (I'd heard a rumor that she actually *had* a Naughty List . . . and you did *not* want to be on it.) "I thought you weren't trying out." She shook her finger at me and tsk-tsked, like I was in trouble for not telling her I was coming.

"I changed my mind," I said with a shrug. "I'm here to support my friends more than anything, I guess."

Skylar gave me a funny look. "Well, I hope you do great. You'd be a perfect captain for next year."

"Actually," I said, speaking quietly, hoping no one would overhear me, "there are a few other people trying out today who would be perfect for captain next year. And they'd be amazing on the team this year too, of course."

"Really?" Skylar asked, arching one eyebrow. "You have some ideas for who should be captain, but . . . you're not talking about you?"

"Not me," I said. "Obviously, Sylvie or Heidi would be great captains next year. . . ." I smiled, trying to sound like I meant it. I knew both of my best friends would *love* to be captain of the dance team. And because I sort of knew Skylar, I knew it was my best-friend duty to tell her how great they were right before auditions. It never hurt to be top-of-mind, as my dad always says.

But even still, I found it hard to feel sincere, since I knew I'd feel *really* left out if one or both of my best friends were captains of the dance team next year, when I wasn't even on the team. Then I thought about what my dad and I had talked about, and tried to swallow back my pride—it felt like I was trying to slurp down a giant ice cube that kept getting stuck in my throat. Then I added, "But do you know Ava Young?"

Skylar shook her head. "No."

"She's an amazing dancer. She's pretty quiet most of the time in school, but once you get to know her, she's not at all shy. She'd be an incredible captain." I looked over to the gym door, and saw that Ava had just walked in. Bailey and a few other girls were with her, and they were all laughing. Ava looked nervous, but I knew she'd rock as soon as her music came on. "That's her," I said, pointing as subtly as I could.

"Are you being serious?" Skylar asked, putting her hands on her hips. I turned back to look at her. "Why do you sound like a commercial? What does this girl have on you?"

I could feel my face getting hot, and I squirmed under Skylar's gaze. "Nothing! I just thought you should know how good she is," I muttered. "Watch Ava carefully, because she's your star."

"*O-kay*," Skylar said suspiciously. She rolled her eyes, as though it were seriously insane that I was trying to talk up my friends. I guess maybe it seemed a little out of character. "Whatever you say, Izzy." She smiled, then patted my shoulder. I suddenly felt really stupid. It wasn't like an endorsement from me was going to get Ava a spot on the team—or would it? As I walked back to Heidi and Sylvie, I realized that telling Skylar how great Ava is wasn't going to *hurt* her, at least.

"What were you talking to Skylar about?" Heidi asked, as she stretched her hamstrings.

"I was just telling her that I knew a few people who would make great captains next year," I singsonged.

"Us?" Sylvie squealed.

"Of course," I said, feeling a little guilty when I saw how happy they both looked. Was it bad that I'd been *slightly* more enthusiastic when I'd talked about Ava's skills than I was when I'd talked about Heidi or Sylvie? I was pretty sure it was okay. Heidi and Sylvie were popular, so they didn't really need my help as much as Ava did. "You know I think you guys are gonna be great today."

"I have a feeling you'll be great too," Sylvie said, pulling me in for a hug. "I'm glad you're here, Iz."

"Of course I'm here!" I said, swatting her. "I'd be here no matter what. The messed-up thing is that I'm actually trying out." I bit my lip, realizing just how many people were still flooding into the gym.

"Ugh," Heidi said, tugging the bottom of her shirt down over the top of her shorts. "I think half the school is here. Mostly girls. I don't think Henry or Jake or Liam or any of the other guys came to watch, but still . . . ugh."

Heidi, Sylvie, and I all stood in a line, surveying the scene.

I noticed that Bailey had found herself a seat way up at the top of the bleachers with a few other girls I recognized from our grade. She had her video camera out, as usual, and looked ready to record. Ava was stretching on the other side of the gym. She looked my way, and as I lifted my arm to wave, Mrs. Sills—the dance team advisor—turned down the music and shouted for attention.

"Let's get started!" She called, waving her arms in the air. "Take a seat and get comfortable, because we're going to be here for a while." Everyone moved toward the bleachers, looking for somewhere to sit, while Mrs. Sills continued to shout out instructions. "Now remember, everyone has one minute to get their CD or MP3 loaded and get set, and one minute to dance. With almost a hundred of you signed up to try out today, we need to keep things rolling."

Sylvie and Heidi and I slid onto one of the benches toward the bottom of the bleachers. We were right behind the captains and returning dance team members, so I hoped we'd get to overhear their comments. I was so excited to hear what they'd say about Ava after they saw how well she could dance. I glanced over at the other end of our row, and saw that Ava was sitting just a few people over from Heidi.

"Ava!" I called out in a stage whisper when Mrs. Sills

stopped talking to get the tryout list in order. She also set up a video camera right by the head table, so the team could review the dances later when they were making final decisions about the auditions.

Ava looked over at me and waved just the slightest bit.

"Good luck," I mouthed, smiling at her.

She smiled back, and I decided I was definitely doing the right thing. I looked behind me, craning my neck to get a view of the uppermost seats of the bleachers. Bailey was looking down at me, and when I smiled, she smiled back too. *Yes!* I thought. *I'm a reputation-makeover genius.*

The first couple of girls to dance were sixth graders, and they were kind of awful (if I was being honest). One girl completely forgot her steps, and another—who was dancing to the exact same song as the first girl—fell in the middle of her routine. Heidi and Sylvie snickered, but I stayed silent, since I knew I was going to be in the same boat in just a few minutes. I felt bad for them.

As I waited for them to call my name, I got more and more nervous. I clutched at my phone, which I'd cued up to my song, silently hoping they might accidentally skip over me and just move on to Heidi and Sylvie and then everyone else. What was I thinking, trying to make myself "relatable" through humiliation? Maybe, if I'd just given it time, I could have convinced Bailey and Ava that I was trying to be a different person in some other way.

But it was too late now. I'd signed up, and someone was calling my name. I knew I had to try to look like I knew what I was doing, and just hope fake confidence would make people believe I wasn't awful. "Isabella Caravelli!" Mrs. Sills shouted. It took me a few seconds to stand up, which was too many for Mrs. Sills. "Izzy, hop to it. The world doesn't wait for you."

Heidi giggled beside me. I stood up on shaky legs, and made my way to the center of the gym. I stuck my phone into the music player and looked up at everyone who was watching me. Usually, I relished the feeling of being watched, of being talked about, of being admired. But today, it was a totally different feeling. I hated this.

With a quick glance at Ava, I pushed play. My music— the song I'd been practicing dancing to with Ava and Bailey all summer—vibrated out of the speakers. I'd decided to use the same song as Ava, since I was so familiar with it. I didn't think she'd mind. Lots of people used the same songs.

On trembling legs, I moved my body as best I could. I tried so hard to zone out and do the routine I'd practiced with my mom the night before. But it was hard to concentrate on my dance when I could feel the whole world watching me make a total fool of myself! My body went on autopilot, and I blanked out as I felt my body doing *something*. I was sweating more than a normal person should sweat in sixty seconds of dancing, and my hair was stuck in my lip gloss.

I made the fatal error of looking up into the bleachers about halfway through my dance, and I could see that Bailey was whispering something to the girl sitting next to her. Was she talking about me? I focused on staring at nothing instead, but I was obsessing over what people were thinking. I knew I was no Jennifer Lopez, but I seriously hoped I didn't look like one of the really bad audition-round losers on *So You Think You Can Dance*.

When I finished, everyone clapped. Heidi and Sylvie were both smiling in a genuine way, and not a single person was laughing at me.

"So maybe it wasn't *as* terrible as I thought it would be," I whispered to Heidi, when I returned to my seat in the stands. Sylvie had already made her way down to the gym floor to get her music set up. I looked around nervously, trying to gauge what people thought. No one was laughing, so that was a good sign.

"You were fine!" Heidi promised. "That was a fun routine."

"Ava gave me a lot of tips this summer," I said, smiling with relief. I was so glad Bailey and Ava had been willing to teach me some stuff this summer, or I would have looked like a total idiot. "She taught me pretty much everything I know about dancing."

Heidi rolled her eyes, obviously still unimpressed by my summer experience. I'd already come to terms with the fact that maybe Heidi, Sylvie, Bailey, Ava, and I were never going to all be best friends together, but I hoped that in time, Heidi and Sylvie would understand that they were *my* friends, and really great people no matter what.

Everyone quieted down as Sylvie's music started. She looked poised and polished—and super-pretty—but her routine was sort of wooden and a little boring. She was obviously really nervous. But still, she did an okay job. After Sylvie went, it was Heidi's turn. Heidi was adorable in her cute shorts and an even cuter headband, but all of her choreography was sort of off time with the music.

By the time Ava went up to the center of the stage, there hadn't really been anyone who stuck out as a total shoo-in. I really hoped Ava would do as well as I knew she could—if she did, I was almost positive she'd get a spot on the team. Because I knew what she was capable of, I was sure Ava must be one of the best dancers at our school.

She put her CD in—Ava didn't have a phone of her own yet—and pushed play. When the music started, Heidi leaned over and whispered, "Isn't this your music?"

"Yeah," I said, watching Ava start her dance. "I used Ava's song, since it's the only one I've ever really danced to. I figured there'd be a lot of overlap in music."

Sylvie wrapped her arm through mine and nudged me with her knee. "Her routine looks a lot like yours. . . ."

I tried to ignore them, so I could focus on sending Ava good dance vibes. She looked amazing, totally in control of her movements, and her timing was perfect. The end of her routine, the part I'd been trying to figure out all summer, had her landing in a full splits. I knew she was nervous about that part, but she completely nailed it. When she finished, I stood up and cheered louder than anyone.

As I sat back down, Skylar—who was sitting at the judges' table in front of us—turned around and looked at me. She lifted her eyebrows and gave me another weird look. I smiled back, trying to show her how incredible I thought Ava had done.

Suddenly, though, I realized people around me were all whispering about something. Ava, who had been smiling when she finished her routine, now looked totally depressed as she made her way past the judges back to her seat in the bleachers. I watched as she slumped down in her seat. Her usual post-dance flush was missing, and she looked pale and awkward.

"That's so not classy," Heidi muttered—loudly—to the girls who were sitting next to us.

"Pitiful," Sylvie added, with a flip of her hair.

"What?" I asked, confused about why anyone thought Ava's dance was anything other than perfect.

"Come on, Iz," Sylvie said, leaning forward so she could glare at Ava. "She totally stole your routine."

"That's just so sad," Heidi added. "She was good and everything, but it's obvious she just wants to be you. She must have spent all last month watching you."

"No—" I protested. "Her dance was different from mine. I came up with a new one."

Sylvie lifted her eyebrows and said, "Um, Iz? She totally lifted your routine. The whole thing was pretty much exactly like yours."

I gasped. Suddenly, I realized that when my body had

gone on autopilot, I'd accidentally started dancing the second half of Ava's routine instead of my own. I'd performed the dance she'd been working on all summer—the one that she'd taught me.

My cheeks went red as the full impact of what had happened hit me. When I got up in front of everyone, my mind had gone so blank that I must have forgotten the dance I'd choreographed myself. I had obviously performed way more of the one I'd been dancing with Ava all summer instead. I'd planned to use *pieces* of her routine all along—but not enough that anyone should have ever noticed. "It was her routine," I said, my eyes wide. "She didn't steal it from me—"

Heidi cut me off by laughing loudly, putting on enough of a show that everyone would hear her. I'm sure to everyone else in the gym, it seemed like we were sitting there laughing at Ava. Even though *I* wasn't laughing about *anything*, everyone knew I was usually the ringleader when it came to making fun of people. Heidi stopped laughing long enough to say, "Izzy, it's obvious what happened. You don't have to defend her. She's just desperate. It's really sad, actually."

I was beginning to panic. "No—" I spluttered. This wasn't what I'd planned at all. Unfortunately, the more I protested, the angrier and more certain my friends became. They were sure I'd somehow made Ava look like a copycat on purpose, and they were really enjoying watching the fallout.

Because gossip moved at the speed of light, it already seemed like the whole gym was buzzing about how Ava Young had performed a stolen dance. And the whole mess was completely my fault.

Chapter Nineteen

~~~~~~~~~~~~~~~~~~~~~~~~~~~~~~~~

Mrs. Sills shushed us so we could move on with the tryouts. There were still about twenty people who needed to dance, but everyone was totally distracted and fidgety. Everyone was staring at Ava—Heidi and Sylvie had started a trend to glare at her. It was amazing how quickly people could forget that Ava had rocked her dance and remember only that there were way too many pieces of her routine that were suspiciously similar to my choreography. And it wasn't even *my* choreography! My choreography was just a bad version of *Ava's* choreography.

I was relieved when Mrs. Sills told us that tryouts would be canceled and no one would make the team if we couldn't calm down. At least then people were forced to stop talking about Ava. But even though no one was talking about it anymore, I didn't like that I had to sit quietly and just let people think what they were thinking about her. She hadn't copied me!

I told Heidi and Sylvie over and over again that they had it all wrong, but for some reason everyone found that impossible to believe. Once rumors and gossip started, it was almost impossible to keep it from snowballing into a giant avalanche.

When the last dancer finished her routine, Skylar announced that they'd be posting the team list in the morning before school. "The returning dance team members will be gathering at my house tonight to discuss the auditions. We need to figure out who will be an asset on our team for this year and who will need to try again next year. But just know, you were all incredible," she said, insincerely. "I love the amount of originality we saw in this year's routines." Then she looked around and I saw her catch Ava's eye in the crowd. Ava looked down, then rushed toward the doors as people began to stand up to leave.

I chased after her. "Ava!" I yelled, hoping she'd hear me over the din of activity in the gym. "Ava, wait!"

But Ava didn't wait—she just twisted through the groups

of girls (and a few guys) who were crowding the door of the gym and made her way outside. I ran through the gym doors and pushed through the crowds into the front hall. Bailey hustled past me, also trying to catch Ava as she fled.

"Bailey!" I grabbed Bailey's arm as she passed. She would understand. If I told her my plan, my stupid *stupid* plan, she'd get it. She had to.

But Bailey shrugged me off, then pushed my hand away. "I can't believe you did that," she hissed. "You stole Ava's routine and intentionally humiliated her."

"That's not what I was trying to do," I said. "I promise."

"Your promises are completely fake," Bailey said. "You make a lot of promises, but then you just go back to the same old tricks."

"With everyone staring at me, I blanked. I didn't plan to do the same dance." I told Bailey the same thing I'd said to both Heidi and Sylvie a million times already. "But anyway, I'm a terrible dancer. Ava's amazing. Everything I did, she did a lot better." Bailey narrowed her eyes at me and I barreled on. "Anyway, I didn't mean for this to happen. I wanted to—"

Bailey cut me off. "Unfortunately, Izzy, you got *exactly* what you wanted. You somehow managed to ruin Ava's most important day and make yourself look better. She spent all summer practicing for this audition." She stopped, choked up for a second. "You *know* how hard she worked for this, because you were there. But you totally backstabbed her. She taught you everything she knows, and you used it to your own advantage. That's just mean. You're just—"

Bailey almost looked like she was going to cry. I could tell she was angry, but I could also tell she was really hurt. But instead of crying, which would have probably been the normal thing to do, she pushed me. Hard.

I stumbled backward, then fell to the ground. As I toppled over, I knocked into a couple of girls' legs. Someone gasped, then I heard someone else say, "What a freak." As Heidi and Sylvie ran up behind me, Bailey turned and fled. People stared after her, but Bailey just shoved through the crowds to escape. Ava was already long gone, and I knew she was going after her—to comfort her, to make her feel better after what I'd done.

Heidi ran up to me and held out her hand so I could stand up. I brushed off my shorts and bent down to massage my knee. It was really throbbing. Heidi's mouth hung open, staring off in the direction Bailey had gone. "I can't believe that psychopath just pushed you over. She's completely crazy."

"Yeah," Sylvie agreed. She went to work fixing my hair so I didn't look like someone who'd just spent the last few seconds on the nasty floor outside the gym. "That girl reminds me of one of those psycho stalkers, the ones who chase after celebrities and, like, try to sneak into their houses just so they can hurt them. You see stories about that stuff in magazines and on TMZ all the time. She's obviously so obsessed with you that she had to push you down."

I listened to them talk about Bailey, wishing I could stop the horrible gossip train that was already zooming along, full speed ahead. I tried to find the words to convince them that they were totally mixed up, that *I* was the one who was becoming obsessed with Bailey and Ava, and that I loved hanging out with them. And that *I'd* been the one who'd stolen *Ava's* routine, that I'd auditioned just so I could convince her and Bailey that I was "relatable" and (maybe?) a worthwhile friend. My plan was obviously faulty, and it was becoming clear that no one would believe me, no matter what I said.

I had a reputation, and I was obviously living up to it.

I had no idea what I was going to have to do to prove that I hadn't meant to humiliate Ava. My knee throbbed, but I barely even felt it. All I felt was sad. As I stood in the hall, surrounded by a mess of people who were all cooing and fretting over me, I wondered: Was it even possible to convince people I'd changed, or was I better off just giving up to play the mean girl forever?

It was in Heidi's mom's car, halfway to my house, that I thought of an idea. The idea was maybe a little crazy, but I figured it was worth it. I needed to fix what I'd done, and I'd never been the kind of girl who was happy to just sit around and whimper over a misunderstanding. And that's all this whole mess was . . . a misunderstanding. I had the power to change people's minds, and that's what I was going to do. Whether or not I'd succeed was a whole other matter, but at least I could *try*!

Because auditions had gone on for so long, it was almost seven o'clock when Heidi's mom dropped me off at my house. I knew I had to hurry if I wanted to have any hope of putting my plan into action. So I ran inside, changed into jeans and a black long-sleeved T-shirt, and found my dad. He was working in his study, but I hoped he'd take pity on me and help out. After all, it was his crappy advice that had gotten me into this mess . . . sort of.

"Dad," I said, knocking lightly before I walked into his office. "Can you drive me over to Bailey's house?"

He looked up at me, bleary-eyed. "What? Now?"

"Yes, now." I picked at my fingernail. Then I smiled. "Please?"

He ran his hand through his hair and stood up. "I trust this has something to do with the image makeover we talked about?"

"Unfortunately, yes. That whole 'make yourself relatable' thing? It's not going quite as well as I might have hoped it would."

"Well, then," he said, walking toward me. "I'm happy to help with both setup *and* cleanup—that's my job, after all. Let's hit the road."

As we ran out the front door, my mom stopped us. "How did it go?"

I cringed. "Not great. Kinda crappy, actually."

Mom looked at me strangely for a second. I waited for her to scold me for being negative or using bad grammar or *something*. But, instead, she shrugged and smiled. "At least you tried, right? That's better than nothing."

"Yeah," I agreed, matching her grin. "At least I tried."

At Bailey's house, Dad waited in the car while I ran up and rang the doorbell. The house was dark, but I waited a minute, just in case. "Isabella?" My dad called from the open passenger-door window, right when I was about to give up. "I just remembered that Erica is traveling this week. Bailey is staying with a friend."

As I ran back to the car, I muttered, "You could have told me that before we drove over here. . . ." But I said nothing when I got back in the car. I figured it wasn't such a great idea to get in a fight with my dad on the very same night two of my most important friends already hated me.

We pulled up at Ava's house a few minutes later. All the lights were on, which gave me hope. I ran up to the door after begging my dad to stay in the car. But I knew if I was gone for long, he'd definitely go inside to chat with Ava's dad. Hopefully, it wouldn't be too hard to pry him away from social hour when the time came to go to phase two of my plan to fix things. I seriously hoped this plan would go over better than all my other plans had, since I was on a real losing streak.

Madeline answered the door. She gave me a look that made me pretty certain she knew what had happened at tryouts earlier, but she led me to Ava's room anyway. She walked ahead of me, with her hands on her hips. The door to Ava's room was open, and I could hear Bailey's voice before I could see either of them inside.

"I'm glad you're both here," I said, as I stood in the doorway. I leaned against the door frame to hold me up, since I felt like I was wilting with nerves. "I need to talk to both of you." I squared my shoulders and tried to convey strength and determination, but instead I felt sick to my stomach. I was reminded of that first day at the resort, when I'd felt like such an outcast with everyone staring at me. But this time, I knew, I had more to lose, and I couldn't just walk away and hide out by myself if they didn't want to take me back.

"We don't want to hear what you have to say," Bailey said, crossing her arms. She was sitting on Ava's bed, with her back against the wall. Ava was on the floor. Her hair was wet, as though she'd just gotten out of the shower, and she was stretching.

"I want to play a game of Liar and Spy, if you don't mind. I'm going to tell you three things," I said the exact words I'd rehearsed in my head on the drive over to Ava's house. But as I spoke, I realized I'd sounded a lot more eloquent in my head—out loud, I sounded sort of silly. And my voice was shaking. "You need to figure out if I'm telling you the truth, or if I'm lying."

Bailey narrowed her eyes and twisted her hair up into a messy pile on top of her head. Without even paying attention to what she was grabbing, she pulled a toothbrush off Ava's cluttered bedside table and pushed it into her curls to hold the hair in place. I glanced at Ava and knew from the look on her face that we'd both seen what had just happened.

It was impossible not to laugh at the total grodiness of the situation, so I cracked a smile. But when I tried to smile at Ava, to share the humor, she averted her eyes. "Fine," she said, still refusing to look at me. She looked at Bailey and shrugged. Bailey rolled her eyes. "But you better respect the game."

I took a deep breath, nodded, then said, "First statement: Ava, you were—without question—the best dancer who tried out today."

"That's true," Bailey said, "but—"

"Just wait," I begged, holding up my hand. I took a step so I was just inside Ava's room. Madeline was still lurking around behind me in the hall, listening to everything. "The second thing I have to say is, today was supposed to be really embarrassing . . . for me. I choreographed a routine of my own, but when I got up in front of everyone, my body just sort of went numb. I didn't mean to use your routine." I chewed on my lip and waited for Ava to say something. She just stared down at her lap.

I continued on, hoping they'd believe me. "The whole

reason I tried out today was to show some support for my friends—Ava, Heidi, Sylvie, everyone—and to try to prove to both of you that I'm trying to change. You guys *know* that I don't like to do anything that might possibly embarrass me, and you *also* know that I'm a hopeless dancer. I guess what I was hoping would happen today was that you would see that I'm not always so obsessed with my own image and reputation. I wanted to be there to support you, and if I looked stupid, who cares?"

I stopped to take a breath, because I could hear myself yammering. On, and on, and on. I had to get to the point. Suddenly, the point sounded really lame, though. "The bottom line is, I wasn't trying to embarrass Ava, or to make people think she'd stolen my routine. Honestly, my version of your dance was such a mess that I'm surprised anyone even noticed that the choreography was the same. But I know I messed up, and everything got carried away, and I'm sorry!" I sucked in a huge breath, then blew it out, yoga-style.

Bailey lifted her eyebrows. "Was that all one story? Because it sounded like a lot of *blah-blah-blah*. Are we supposed to guess if it's the truth or a lie?"

"Now you guess," I said, shrugging. "But I'll give you a clue: It's not a lie."

Ava tucked her legs under her body and looked at me—finally. "I believe you."

"You do?" Bailey and I said this at the same time.

"I do believe you," Ava said. "I think you're telling the truth, Izzy. But I think what you did was really badly thought out and you must have had at least some idea that it was going to backfire." She looked at me and fussed with her bangs. "Or maybe you didn't. But I don't know why you thought trying out for the dance team was going to get us to think you were suddenly this nice person who thinks of others before you think of yourself."

"And anyway," Bailey said, cutting in. "It doesn't matter what you *meant* to have happen, since the only thing that *did* happen after your little performance today was that Ava looked like a copycat. She's never going to make the dance team now, since people think she stole her routine from you and not the other way around." She whipped the toothbrush out of her hair, shook her curls down around her shoulders, and studied the long piece of plastic in her hand. "Ew. Sorry about that, Ava." She tossed the toothbrush across the room, where it landed in the wastebasket.

I took another step into the room. "The third thing I wanted to say is, I really do think of the two of you as good friends—some of my best friends, even. And I don't want to lose you, just because we're back at school and I'm known as this 'mean girl' or whatever." I cringed, then carried on. "I hate that people think I'm a bad person, and I'm sad that I've done so many things to hurt people's feelings over the past few years. I want to change my reputation, and I know it's going to take some time. But I really need *you* to believe me when I say that I'm trying. I need someone to believe I *can* change." I shrugged. "Also, I need your help to try to undo the mess I made today."

Bailey studied me carefully. "Truth?"

"Yep. I promise not to lie to you." I really, really meant it—even though saying something so earnest made me feel like a major dork.

"So what do you need our help with?" Ava asked quietly.

"Wait," Bailey said, folding her legs under her body on the bed. "So you're good, Ava? You're just going to forgive Izzy, just like that?"

"Friends forgive," Ava said, shrugging. "She's telling us the truth, she meant well—what's done is done. We move on."

Bailey pouched out her lips and squinted. "Okay. We move on. In that case, sorry I smacked you to the ground, Iz. That was sort of a heat-of-the-moment thing. My body went all crazy on me, and I just needed to hit someone."

"Classy." I said, laughing. "I admire your passion."

"I'll try not to let it happen again. Friends forgive, but friends also ought not to shove friends onto the spit-soaked school atrium floor. That was nasty."

After a moment, where I let it sink in—that this was happening, they were forgiving me, and they believed me—I whispered, "Thank you. For everything."

"You bet. So?" Bailey blurted out. "You said you have something planned that you want our help with. What is it?"

"The Spy part of Liar and Spy," I said. "Who's up for a mission?"

Ava grinned. "Me."

"Me too," Bailey said.

"We have a little prep to do first," I said, flying into high gear. "Bailey, get out your video camera. Ava, prepare to be sneaky and swift. If this is going to work, we need to move fast. . . ."

Chapter Twenty

Thanks to Ava's dad's humongous iMac and all of his super-user-friendly design and video editing software, Bailey's prep for our spy mission was complete in less than fifteen minutes. We ran back to the car, pulling my dad (who couldn't resist the opportunity to come in and chat) along behind us like a paid driver. The three of us squeezed into the backseat in our matching jeans and black shirts, then I told my dad where to drive, and we were off.

On the way, Bailey and Ava and I went through all the possible land mines for our operation, but I think we all knew that we had no idea what we were in for until we actually saw what was happening at Skylar's house. I knew we'd have to improvise as the night went along, but it still felt good to talk through some of the potential challenges. At the very least, it made the drive go faster. Skylar lived on the other side of the lake from me, in one of the *super*-fancy houses that lined the creek. It wasn't all that far, actually, but the streets wound around in these confusing and twisty circles and one-ways, so we kept getting lost.

"What if there's a security gate?" Bailey asked while Dad backed out of a dead-end street.

"We climb over it," Ava said, as though it was simple as that.

"There isn't a security gate," I added. "I've seen her house before."

"What happens if they've already watched the audition videos?" Bailey wondered.

"Auditions have only been over for an hour. I hope they haven't started reviewing the video yet, but if they have, we go to Plan B."

"Which is?" Ava asked.

"We'll figure it out," I said. "I can be a sweet-talker when I need to be."

"What if she has one of those attack dogs?" Ava asked, nervously pushing her hair away from her face. "The kind who get their own sign on the front window of the house—

the signs that basically tell you your arm will be chewed off and turned into doggy hamburger if you go near little poochie poo."

"Unlikely," Bailey said, sounding all business. "You only have to look at Skylar to know she doesn't have a killer dog. If anything, she has a yapper. A poofball who probably poops on a pad in the corner of its very own bedroom. And one of those high-maintenance freaks of nature might be even more trouble than a killer." Bailey pulled a small mirror out of her sweatshirt pocket and began to apply black eyeliner to the skin all around her eyes. "It's going to bark to give up our location."

"What's with the black eyes?" I asked, watching as she pressed the tip of her mom's obviously expensive eyeliner against the apples of her cheeks.

She looked at me like I was the crazy one. "Spyware. Don't spies usually slather their eye sockets in black so they're less noticeable?" Bailey returned to her coloring project.

"Um, actually, don't they only do that when they're wearing one of those full face masks with the eyeholes? That way, the light skin around the eyes won't be as visible. But black around the eyes *without* the mask just makes you look like a raccoon."

"Oh well," Bailey said. She jabbed the cap back on the eye pencil, its end blunt and useless now. "I like the way it looks, and anyway, my part of the plan is done—this way, I'll feel like I'm actually in the action instead of just the ace prep team whose job now is to stay as quiet and out of the way as possible."

"You were an excellent ace prep team," I offered, in a British accent. "Top-notch, really."

"Why thank you, Spiz."

"Spiz?" I said, giggling.

Bailey snorted. "Spy Iz. It's a name mash-up, like Brenley."

Ava laughed so hard and loud that my dad actually hit the brakes and sent us all flying forward into locked seat belts. "Is Brenley a mash-up of Bailey and Brennan? Aw . . . it could be your first kid's name. Auntie Spiz, meet baby Brenley." She giggled. "What can we call me?"

I thought for a sec, then blurted out, "Snava."

Ava was now laughing so hard she could hardly even breathe. "*Snava?*"

"Sneaky Ava," I explained. "You *are* the best creeper and sneaker in our game of Spy. You're the only one who can get through the woods without sounding like a bear or a moose."

"Am I supposed to be the moose in that example?" Bailey

screeched. "I wasn't that loud when we were spying on Brennan. I can be quiet." After a moment, she added, "Sometimes."

"Should I be worried about you girls' safety?" My dad asked, glancing at us in the rearview mirror. We'd told him nothing about our plan since we'd left Ava's house, and he'd been respectful enough not to ask many questions. But now I'm sure our conversation was starting to cross over into the concerned parent realm. It was fair for him to ask a few questions, I guess, since he was the one driving us around on our mission.

Still laughing about Brenley and Snava and Spiz, I told him no, that what we were doing was perfectly legal (if you didn't count the breaking and entering) and would lead to nothing more than a little (okay, a lot of) embarrassment if we were to get caught.

Moments later, Dad pulled up in front of the house two doors down from Skylar's and turned off the car lights. "I assume I'm supposed to keep a low profile out here?" He turned in his seat to look at us and lifted his eyebrows. "Anything else I need to know, as your getaway vehicle driver?"

I smiled at him, a quick gesture of thanks as we piled out of the car. "We'll be back in ten minutes, hopefully," I said. "But don't worry if it's more like twenty."

"You're not toilet-papering this girl's house, are you?" Dad asked quietly, out the open drivers' side window. "I'm not sure that's such a cool thing to do these days."

"Not TP-ing, Dad," I promised. "Just trying to get Ava a much-deserved spot on the dance team. It's all good, nothing bad. Promise." I paused. "You trust me, right?"

He smiled. "I do." Then he did this elaborate hand signal and whistled. "Well, good luck, and I'll see you on the flip side."

We all giggled, then slipped through Skylar's neighbor's lawn and hid behind the row of neatly trimmed bushes that seemed to divide all of the lawns in this part of town. The hedges were about neck-high—unless you were Ava, and then they were too tall to see over.

"Entry point?" Ava asked, looking up at Bailey and me for guidance.

"Looks like we're going to have to squeeze around to the back," I said, noticing that the lights in most of the front of the house were dark. There was one lamp on in the corner of the living room, and I'm pretty sure I saw old-man slippers perched on an ottoman. In my mind that meant one thing: parent space, not dance team hangout area.

We crept around the side of the house, snaking along the

ground whenever we had to go under a window. We would have looked completely ridiculous to an outside observer, but (hopefully) no one was watching. So we just kept slipping and soft-stepping and sneaking our way along the side of the house.

Just as we were about to round the corner, something hissed—and moments later, I was hit full in the face with a spray of water. "Sorry!" Bailey called, in her too-loud voice. "I did that. Hose on! My bad."

Ava and I both shushed her. Bailey leaned over to turn off the hose—and, in turn, the attached sprinkler—that she'd accidentally turned on when she'd brushed against the side of the house.

I was soaked, head to toe. As we made our way past the privacy fence (there was a simple, unlocked gate that led into the backyard), I discovered that when I walked, I now made slurching sounds with each step. "I can't sneak into Skylar's house sopping wet," I said. "I'll leave puddles and a huge mess."

"Also, it sort of sounds like you're farting with each step you take, so . . ." Bailey laughed at her own joke. "Yeah. Izzy can't go in. And we already know *I* can't go in, since I'll probably just knock something over or stub my toe and scream or something. We can't trust me with any project that's supposed to be quiet and stealthy."

Ava nodded. "I guess that leaves me: Snava. I am prepared for my mission." We were crouched in a corner of Skylar's backyard, hidden under the swaying branches of a smallish willow tree. A sliding glass door from the walkout basement led to a brick patio, which ended where the lawn began. We were about twenty feet from the door, with a full view of the basement. On the other side of the glass, six girls were getting comfortable on a huge cushy sectional in front of the TV. Skylar had a DVD in her hand, and as we watched, she leaned down and slid it into the DVD player under the TV.

"We need to create a distraction so Ava can get in there without being seen," I said. "Now." I jumped up and skittered out from under the tree. "If you see an opening, go!"

Without thinking, I ran back through the gate and around the side of the house. Hurriedly, I pressed the doorbell, waited five seconds, then pressed it again. When no one answered, I pressed it again.

Finally, Skylar's dad came to the door. "Hello, sir," I said, in my best teachers-and-parents voice. "I was wondering if I could have a word with Skylar?"

"Oh, uh . . ." The guy was obviously confused. "Are you one of the dance girls?"

"Sure," I said, shrugging. "I just need to talk to her for a sec."

Skylar's dad stepped away from the door and yelled down the stairs. I held my breath as I waited, beginning to shiver as the water from the sprinkler soaked through my clothes and rubbed my skin. My hair hung in wet black sheets around my shoulders and drizzled trails of water down my shirt.

Moments later, Skylar appeared at the top of the stairs and made her way to the front door. "Hi, Izzy," she said, trying to sound friendly and cheerful, but I could hear the undertone of suspicion layered in her voice too. "What's up?"

"Um," I said, flying by the seat of my pants. Why hadn't I thought about how to create a diversion? I'd only thought about how to talk our way out of things if we were caught. "I just—um, I just, uh, wanted to apologize for today and let you know that . . ." I had to pick my words carefully, careful not to repeat any of the things I'd already said on Bailey's DVD—the DVD that we needed to get into Skylar's house. "Actually!" I said, brightening. I tried to infuse my voice with confidence, to not let Skylar see me sweat. "I was just wondering if—"

Skylar cut me off. "Why are you so wet?" She crinkled up her nose. "And I think you have a piece of tree in your hair."

"Yeah," I said, trying to laugh it off. "Just out for a run. You know, soccer training and all." I grinned, switching subjects. "Anyway, I was wondering if I could, um, apologize to everyone for being so . . ." Oy. My mom would have me sent to speech therapy if she could hear how eloquently I was fumbling my way through this performance. "For being so, um, disruptive today. And, um, not very good. I'm disappointed in myself." I pouted, trying to play up the sympathy angle.

"I can let them know you stopped by," Skylar said, starting to give me a look I was all too familiar with, since it was one of my own "you're a freak" looks.

"No," I said, reaching out to hold the door open. "Can you just call them up here for a few seconds?"

Now Skylar was *really* looking at me like I was insane. I was acting crazy, sure, but I was acting like this to salvage Ava's reputation. It was worth every stupid thing I had to say if I could distract them long enough for Ava to do her thing. She just needed a minute or two to sneak into Skylar's house, replace the DVD in the player, and get back out again without being seen.

"Listen, I know it's unconventional, but . . ." I ran a hand through my hair and shrugged. "Could I just dance for you one more time?" I swallowed back the huge lump of embarrassment that was clogging up my throat.

"You want to . . . dance? For me? One more time?" A slow smile crept over Skylar's face. She knew this whole scene had total humiliation (for me, obviously) written all over it. I could tell she was seriously considering letting me dance for her again, just because it would be hilarious. I knew if I were in her position, I'd totally want to see someone make a fool out of themselves by begging for something that I was in the position to give. "If you really want to," Skylar said slowly. "Come on in."

"No!" I said, sounding panicky. "I need some extra space, so, um . . . maybe I could dance out here, in the yard?" Oh, oh, oh, *what* was I doing? I seriously hoped this would work. "Can you call the other girls up, and you guys can, like, make a little audience around me?"

Skylar's smile widened, but then she pulled her eyebrows together. "Izzy, are you sure you want to do this? You know it kind of looks like begging . . . which is sort of pitiful." She was giving me an out. She knew that if I really did this—danced for the dance team members on the lawn outside Skylar's house—I was setting myself up as the joke of the night. Joke of the month, probably. She was giving me the chance to walk away, to keep this between us, and save myself the embarrassment of humiliating myself in front of the whole team. But I didn't have much choice, since I had to get them all out of that basement room somehow.

"I know," I said, swallowing back my pride. "It's okay. Yes, I'm sure. I really want to do this."

Skylar studied me for a second, then said, "Okay. I guess if you really want to dance for us one more time, I'm not going to stop you. It takes—I don't *know* what to come over here and beg for another chance."

She went inside, and a few minutes later, returned to the front lawn with the rest of the dance team. Obviously, Skylar had already filled them in on what was happening, since they all looked at me strangely when they came outside. A few of them were giggling. "Hi, guys," I said, stalling for time. I hoped Ava was making her way to the sliding glass door at that very moment. "I just wanted to, um, dance for you one more time. Show you my skills. So thanks for coming, and— here goes."

I backed up, trying not to look at anyone's face as I started to shimmy and dance on the lawn. I tried to remember my own performance this time, but my body didn't seem to be willing to cooperate. I knew I looked bad, but it was all in the name of friendship. I heard a few giggles, but I focused on doing as much of my routine as I could remember without the music giving me cues. The whole mess of a routine took less than a minute—but I knew that would probably be more than enough time for Ava to complete our spy mission.

When I finished, I put my hands up in the air and smiled. The girls from the dance team stared at me, as I thought they would. Two or three of them clapped, but I could tell it was just to make me feel less awkward. It didn't help.

"Well," Skylar said after a moment. "That was . . . interesting."

I blushed. "Thanks. I also just wanted to say that I know I'm probably not in the running for actually *making* the team." Skylar lifted her eyebrows. "And that's totally fine—I know I'm not a great dancer. I just wanted to, you know, give it my best shot. So, I, uh, I've done that now, and I guess I'll be on my way!" My voice had gotten high and squeaky, a side effect of the embarrassment, I guess.

"Izzy?" Skylar said, stepping forward. "This whole thing was really random. You know that, right?"

I nodded. "Yeah. Hey, before you guys go back inside, I

just wanted to say—keep an open mind about the auditions, okay? And enjoy the video!"

"O-*kay*," Skylar said slowly. "Have a good night."

The girls all looked at me one last time before they went back inside. As soon as the front door shut behind them, I took a huge breath and blew it out. Then I hustled around the side of the house to rejoin my friends.

When I slipped through the gate and tucked back in under the willow tree, Ava gave me a thumbs-up. "Whatever you did, worked. I had enough time to get in there and swap out the video. I was back out here before anyone saw me!"

I grinned and crouched down. "Let's stick around to see what happens."

As we watched, the dance team settled in on the couch again. I could tell they were all laughing, which wasn't all that surprising since they'd just witnessed me humiliating myself—big-time—on the front lawn. This was definitely one of those times when I didn't want anyone to be talking about me, since I knew it wasn't good. But I was pretty sure it would be worth it.

A moment later, Skylar leaned over and pushed play on the DVD player. My face came up on the huge flat-screen TV. I looked pretty good! "Hi!" I could see my mouth saying.

"Before you rewatch today's tryouts and make your selections for this year's dance team, please watch this short video. For the record, Ava Young did not steal my routine—regardless of what people may have said and thought. I stole her dance, and this video will prove that to you. She deserves all the credit for her choreography. And also, she's an awesome teacher and would make an amazing future captain. Sit back and enjoy."

I saw Skylar's mouth drop open in disbelief. All the girls in the basement started talking at once, confused about what was going on. I'm sure the whole situation was made even more confusing because I'd been on the lawn—dancing like a dying chicken—less than a minute earlier. And now here I was, on Skylar's TV screen.

Ava turned to me and smiled. "I hope they keep watching."

"After what I just did to distract them upstairs . . . ," I muttered, "so do I."

Bailey's pieced-together video played on, and slowly, the dance team girls stopped talking and actually started watching our mini-movie. The video was choppy and quickly edited, but we'd managed to cobble together a two-minute recap of Ava's summer of dancing. In the video, we included a ton of clips showcasing Ava's amazing dance skills, but we also sprinkled in some good scenes where she was teaching me what she knew. The bits from early in the month, where I danced like a wet rag, were especially hilarious and made it obvious that Ava would *never* copy my dancing. The dance team girls watched through to the end. I knew we'd done what we could to make sure they could see that Ava truly was a great dancer.

When the video ended, Skylar got up and went over to the DVD player. She pushed the eject button and studied the DVD carefully. Then she pulled another video off the top of the DVD player and pushed it into the machine. A moment later, the first dancer from the afternoon's auditions was dancing on-screen.

"Well," I said, coming out of my crouch. "I think we've done what we can do."

"If we were true spies"—Bailey scratched her cheek, smearing the black-eye eyeliner across her temple—"we would stick around and try to listen to their discussion about the auditions."

We all looked at each other. "I think I'd rather not know what they say," Ava said softly.

"You and me both," I said, cringing. "So now we wait."

Ava nodded. "Now we wait."

Chapter Twenty-One

～～～～～～～～～～～

When it was time for the list to be posted the next morning, there were dozens of girls packed around the bulletin board outside the school office. Everyone was buzzing about who would get a slot. There were even a few people hanging around who I didn't even remember from tryouts the day before—I think they were just curious onlookers who liked the drama or something.

"What if we all get a spot?" Heidi whispered, nervously chewing her lip. "Can you even imagine?"

"It would be so amazing," Sylvie agreed. She turned to me and squealed. "I'm just so glad you changed your mind and decided to try out, Iz. It will be a million times better with all three of us on the dance team together."

I tried to smile but couldn't. I knew I wasn't going to get a spot. That would be totally insane. But Heidi and Sylvie had no idea what I'd done the night before. The word hadn't yet gotten out about my weird stunt on Skylar's lawn. It *would* get out (I definitely knew how gossip worked, since I was usually the source), but it hadn't yet. When it did, it would be interesting to see how everyone would respond. I was ready for whatever happened. I think.

Skylar pushed through the crowds of people. "Excuse me!" she crooned. "I have the list!" Everyone moved to the side, and Skylar marched past. She slowly unfolded a piece of paper. Then she pulled some tape out of her bag and affixed it to the corners of the paper very slowly and carefully. It felt like it was taking forever, and my heart was beating like crazy in my chest.

Finally . . . it was up on the board and the names of the dance team were right there, in black letters on a pale-pink piece of paper. I scanned the list, but the words all blurred together into a bunch of smeared ink in front of my eyes. Beside me, Sylvie squealed. "I made it!" she said, grabbing my arm. "That's my name."

My eyes adjusted, and I scanned the list.

"Sylvie!" I cried, seeing her name at the top of the list.

"Yay!" My eyes shifted down, then down again. No Heidi. But finally, there—in the final spot—was the name I was most anxiously looking for:

AVA YOUNG.

My arms filled with goose bumps as I realized what this meant. Ava had made it.

"I didn't get it," Heidi said, slumping beside me. "Neither did Izzy."

"I'm sorry," I said, turning to give Heidi a hug. "I wish you were on the list."

Heidi looked at me suspiciously, like she assumed I really meant I wished *I* was on the list. "This is so embarrassing," she grumbled.

"There were only four spots," I said, putting my arm around her shoulder. "There's really no reason to be embarrassed. Just disappointed."

Sylvie was buzzing with energy next to us. She'd already pulled out her phone to text her mom, and she was chatting with one of the other girls who had made the team. "I feel awful," she said to us through a smile when she took a break from celebrating. "I wish you guys could have made the team too."

"I can't believe that freak Ava Young made it, and we

didn't," Heidi said, leaning into me. In that same moment, Sylvie was whisked away, showered with hugs and congratulations from other people near us. "Ava was awful, and one of us deserved that slot. She stole it, and now I think we should make her pay."

"She was not awful, and you know it," I said, annoyed. "She was one of the best dancers out there, and it would have been a big mistake if they'd left her off the team."

Heidi scoffed, saying nothing.

"Seriously, Heidi. Lay off. You're just bitter, and it's not nice. You sound mean and jealous."

Heidi's eyes bugged out at me. Between yesterday and today, I think I'd made my point.

Suddenly, I spotted Ava making her way up to the front of the crowd. Because she was so tiny, she couldn't see over anyone. So she had to get right up to the front before she could see the list. I watched as her eyes scanned the four typed names, then I saw her body tense as she realized she was looking at her own name. I smiled.

"So maybe she wasn't *that* bad," Heidi said, watching me watch Ava. "I guess she was actually pretty good, wasn't she?"

I nodded.

"She really didn't steal your dance?" Heidi said quietly.

"And you didn't plan that whole thing to try to embarrass her and ruin her chances?"

I shook my head. "That dance was all hers, and I'm really, truly happy she made the team. Ava's amazing."

"I don't know if I'd go that far," Heidi said, shrugging.

I laughed. "Someday, maybe we can all hang out, and you can see for yourself."

"Let's not get any crazy ideas, okay?" Heidi said. Then her expression brightened and she added, "But I guess it wouldn't hurt to be sort of nice to her, now that she's on the dance team."

"Oh, Heidi," I said, rolling my eyes. "Just stop."

"What?" she said, shrugging. "It's true. Admit it—you were thinking the same thing."

Three months ago, I probably would have been thinking the same thing. But now, it surprised me to realize that the thought hadn't even crossed my mind. Unfortunately, other people would probably assume I was only being nice to Ava now because she was on the dance team—but they'd have to get over it. Because that wasn't it at all.

"No, actually, I wasn't thinking that." I looked at Heidi and said, "But I was thinking that it would be awesome if you were nice to her just because you want to be. Not because you want something, or because you think she'll do something for you. Just because it's easier than being nasty. Sometimes it's more fun to be nice than it is to be mean. Trust me."

Heidi laughed. "Well, la-di-da, Miss High and Mighty. I hereby nominate you for Miss Congeniality."

I laughed, then looked back at Ava just as she turned away from the list. Her face was flushed, and her eyes searched the crowd. I waved. When she saw me, she gave me a thumbs-up and I gave her one back. Then she turned and walked down the hall with Bailey, who was filming Ava's reaction to making the team.

"Don't you want to go with your new BFFs?" Heidi scoffed, her voice suddenly angry and defensive. "I'm just the loser *old* best friend, the one who *didn't* make dance team. I get it if you need to ditch me. Out with the old, in with the new, right?" She held her head high, but there was something in her voice that made me realize Heidi really *was* scared that I might leave her behind. I suspected she thought both Sylvie and I were going to abandon her, because someone or something better had come along—for me, Ava and Bailey; for Sylvie, the dance team. But I wouldn't do that. Because that would be a different kind of mean, and I wanted to get away from *all* mean.

"I'll find them later," I said, and linked my arm through Heidi's. "For now, I want to hang out with you. We can be sad about not making the team together. And maybe later, we can get some ice cream to dull the pain." I bumped my shoulder against hers and added, "*If* you ditch the mean-girl attitude."

Heidi chewed her lip, then smiled. "I'll try. For you, Isabella Caravelli. Only for you—and ice cream."

I knew life wasn't going to change overnight. I couldn't undo years of a snobby reputation in just a few days. But I knew I was on the right track. Sure, it would take time to show people that I really was trying to be a nicer person. And it would take time to make sure I really *was* being a nicer person.

Maybe some kids in our class would always think of me as the girl who spread rumors about people or the girl who played pranks that hurt people's feelings. And maybe some people would always hold a grudge. Unfortunately, there was nothing I could do to erase what I'd already done except apologize and try to move on.

Some days, I was sure, it would be tempting to slip back into the old routine, just because it was easier to *tease* than it was to *be* teased. And that middle school reality wasn't going to change just because *I* was.

As I walked down the hall, arm in arm with Heidi, I realized one other important thing: maybe Bailey and Ava and I wouldn't necessarily be BFFs back at home . . . but there was always next summer.

In the meantime, I was confident that I could change my attitude *and* my reputation at school. I'd done it once already, this summer. If I set my mind to it, I knew I could do it again.